ARTHUR CONAN DOYLE

The Narrative of
John Smith

EDITED AND WITH AN INTRODUCTION BY
JON LELLENBERG, DANIEL STASHOWER
AND RACHEL FOSS

THE BRITISH LIBRARY

THE EDITORS

Jon Lellenberg, US agent for the Conan Doyle Estate Ltd, is the editor of *The Quest for Sir Arthur Conan Doyle* (1995) and co-editor of the award-winning BBC Radio 4 Book of the Week *Arthur Conan Doyle: A Life in Letters* (2007).

Daniel Stashower is a two-time Edgar Award-winning author whose books include *Teller of Tales: The Life of Sir Arthur Conan Doyle* (1999); *The Beautiful Cigar Girl* (2006) and (as co-editor with Jon Lellenberg) *Arthur Conan Doyle: A Life in Letters* (2007).

Rachel Foss is Lead Curator of Modern Literary Manuscripts at The British Library.

ACKNOWLEDGEMENTS

The Editors wish to thank, for their assistance, Catherine Cooke, Alison Corbett, Susan E. Dahlinger, Michael Dirda, Richard Fairman, Dr Robert S. Katz, Randall Stock and Peter Wood.

First published in 2011 by The British Library
96 Euston Road
London NW1 2DB

British Library Cataloguing-in-Publication Data
A catalogue record for this book is available from The British Library
ISBN 978 0 7123 5841 5

Designed and typeset in Monotype Baskerville by illuminati, Grosmont
Jacket design by Andrew Barron @ thextension
Printed in Hong Kong by Great Wall Printing Co. Ltd

The Narrative of
John Smith

CONTENTS

Bush Villa - Southsea

INTRODUCTION

IN AN ARTICLE called 'My First Book,' published in *The Idler* in January 1893, Arthur Conan Doyle, recounting his struggles as an aspiring young author, referred to an early manuscript which was lost in the post on its way to the publishers. With mock dramatic flourish, he wrote:

> Alas for the dreadful thing that happened! The publishers never received it, the Post Office sent countless blue forms to say that they knew nothing about it, and from that day to this no word has ever been heard of it.

This work was *The Narrative of John Smith*, a novel with a 'personal–social–political complexion' that Conan Doyle undertook during his early years in Southsea, a suburb of Portsmouth, as he attempted to establish himself both as a doctor and as a writer. In June 1881, after five years of study, he had attained his Bachelor of Medicine (MB) and Master of Surgery (CM) from the University of Edinburgh. One year later, after the second of two stints as a ship's surgeon and a short-lived venture as a partner in the Plymouth practice of George Budd, a fellow Edinburgh medical graduate, Conan Doyle arrived in Southsea and rented a house at number 1 Bush Villas, intent on finally making a successful independent start in his chosen profession. 'I took the most central house I could find,' he told a family friend, 'determined to make a spoon or spoil a horn,[1] and got three pounds worth of furniture for the Consulting Room, a bed, a tin of corned beef and two enormous brass plates with my name on it.'[2]

In spite of his qualifications, energy and experience, he faced
a considerable challenge. He was acquainted with neither the
city nor any of its residents, and had practically no money to
cover day-to-day expenses while building up his practice. Family
circumstances only increased the pressure. His father, Charles
Doyle, after suffering failing health and alcoholism for many
years, had been admitted to a 'health resort,' as Conan Doyle
described it, straining the family's already precarious finances. As
the adult son, Conan Doyle was now 'practically the head of a
large struggling family,' and deeply conscious of this responsibility.
'Perhaps it was good for me that the times were hard,' he wrote,
'for I was wild, full-blooded, and a trifle reckless, but the situation
called for energy and application so that one was bound to try
to meet it. My mother had been so splendid that we could not
fail her.'[3] Two of his sisters had taken positions as governesses in
Portugal, sending their pay home, and Conan Doyle was also eager
to contribute to the family's welfare, sending for his ten-year-old
brother Innes and assuming responsibility for him. Conan Doyle's
letters home meticulously detail his efforts and successes on this
score, frequently itemising the particulars of his bills and other
outgoing expenses as well as income gained from medicine and
writing. These letters paint an evocative picture of how precarious
a business it was for him to keep afloat.

By 1884 Conan Doyle was able to report proudly to his mother
that there were more than a hundred Southsea families for whom
he was sole medical adviser. But in 1882 and 1883, patients were
few and far between, and even when an appointment in 1883
as a medical examiner for the Gresham Life Assurance Society
provided some badly needed extra funds, it was primarily writing
that he looked to for additional income. An 1882 letter home makes
clear that, although small at the time, the income from writing
was crucial: 'In the meantime we try to keep the thing going by
literature – yesterday I got the proofs of a photographic article
– not much but a pound I daresay.'[4]

A decade later, Conan Doyle was to abandon medicine in order
to devote himself solely to writing, a decision he later described

as 'one of the great moments of exultation of my life.' But in Southsea he divided his labours and loyalties between medicine and writing, which were sometimes complementary and sometimes antagonistic undertakings. ('It is hard to say which suffered most,' he later joked.)

He had started writing short stories and poetry as a student and regularly tried his luck with magazine submissions. One story in late 1877 or early 1878 was sent to Edinburgh's prestigious *Blackwood's Magazine*. 'The Haunted Grange of Goresthorpe – a True Ghost Story' failed to appear in print, its manuscript sitting in the magazine's archives for many decades unsuspected. His first success came with a story strongly influenced by Edgar Allan Poe: 'The Mystery of Sasassa Valley,' which was published in *Chambers' Journal* on 6 September 1879, earning him the princely sum of three guineas. 'After receiving that little cheque I was a beast that has once tasted blood,' he would tell an interviewer, 'for I knew that whatever rebuffs I might receive – and God knows I had plenty – I had once proved I could earn gold, and the spirit was in me to do it again.' He also started publishing articles, some of them unpaid in the *British Medical Journal* or the *Lancet* to position himself professionally, but also a few paid ones in the *British Journal of Photography*.

He did not allow early rejections of his fiction to discourage him. He took heart from contacts such as James Hogg, editor of the monthly *London Society* and the first of several magazine editors to take an interest in the fledgling writer's work. By 1883, the magazines which had published Conan Doyle included *All the Year Round*, *Blackwood's*, *London Society*, *Chambers' Journal*, *Temple Bar Magazine*, *Good Words* and *Boy's Own Paper*. It was, however, the publication in January 1884 of his story 'J. Habakuk Jephson's Statement' in *The Cornhill* which constituted Conan Doyle's greatest early success. *The Cornhill* was Britain's foremost literary magazine, published by George Smith of Smith, Elder & Co., which had made its name in 1847 with Charlotte Brontë's *Jane Eyre*. Conan Doyle's story's success cemented a budding association with James Payn, an editor he had long admired, and for the first time brought him into the general orbit of London literary society.

His sense of triumph, however, was mingled with frustration owing to the practice of the time, among journals such as *The Cornhill*, of publishing contributions anonymously. In the absence of evidence to the contrary, critics attributed Conan Doyle's story to Robert Louis Stevenson. While proud and flattered by the comparison – Stevenson, like Poe, was a Conan Doyle favourite – it was hardly helpful in his desire to make his name. In *Through the Magic Door*, a book on writers and writing published in 1907, Conan Doyle called this practice 'a most iniquitous fashion by which all chance of promotion is barred to young writers.' With *Habakuk* he realised that short-story writing would not furnish the means to fulfil any serious literary ambition. 'What is necessary is that your name should be on the back of a volume,' he said in an April 1884 letter home: 'Only so do you assert your individuality and get full credit or discredit of your achievement.'[5]

The Narrative of John Smith represents Conan Doyle's first attempt to make the transition from short-story writer to novelist. An 1883 letter points to his growing confidence in his ability to succeed in this venture. He is convinced too of a quality of originality in his work, although less certain whether this originality may produce critical approbation or censure:

> Why should I not have a future before me in letters? I am conscious … of a well marked style of my own which should single me out among the crowd for good or evil, could I only get my head above water.[6]

His self-assurance fluctuated, however, with any belief he had in his technical proficiency tempered by doubt. In an April 1884 letter, he confided to his mother:

> Sometimes I am confident, at others very distrustful. I know I can write small stories in a taking way, but am I equal to a prolonged effort – can I extend a plot without weakening it – can I preserve the identity of a character throughout – these are the questions which vex me.[7]

On the evidence of the *Narrative*, the answer to his questions was a resounding 'no.' There is very little in the way of plot or characterisation: the work is essentially a series of lengthy reflections on contemporary debates occupying the young Conan Doyle in his early twenties. They are voiced by John Smith, a man of fifty who, due to illness, is confined to his rooms for a week. These reflections frequently appear as internal monologues; less frequently, in dialogue between Smith and his doctor, and the other characters who also largely function as extensions of himself. The *Narrative* is not successful fiction, but offers remarkable insight into the thinking and views of a raw young writer who would shortly create one of literature's most famous and durable characters, Sherlock Holmes.

In 1883, when the 23-year-old Conan Doyle was first writing *The Narrative of John Smith*, he had already sold a story that had attracted some critical attention. This was 'The Captain of the "Pole-Star",' a ghost story based upon his Arctic experiences. That spring he had started his novel, but then had the idea for his breakthrough story 'J. Habakuk Jephson's Statement,' based on the Marie Celeste mystery.[8] But when he then returned to and finished his novel, and sent it off to the publisher, the manuscript disappeared forever. 'No I never got poor John Smith,' he told his mother at the beginning of 1884. 'I am going to rewrite him from memory, but my hands are very full just now.'[9]

Smith is presented as a man who has seen much of the world and been many things in life. Now middle-aged, laid up by gout in the boarding-house where he lives, he spends his time conversing with his doctor, landlady, a neighbour and a fellow-lodger who is a retired army major, and ruminating to himself as well, about a variety of matters which constitute the themes of this book. Smith's illness preoccupies him, a topic that flows into broader considerations of medicine, science and human nature. These also connect to discussions of religion, and all relate in various ways to discussions of literature.

Much is semi-autobiographical in nature, Conan Doyle using Smith and the other characters to expound personal views of his own. He had been raised in an intensely Roman Catholic family, and despite scant means his mother had managed to provide him with a very good Jesuit education at Stonyhurst College in Lancashire in the north of England. But while at Stonyhurst he began to renounce the Church in which he had been raised. 'Nothing can exceed the uncompromising bigotry of the Jesuit theology,' he said in his autobiography *Memories and Adventures*:

> I remember that when, as a grown lad, I heard Father Murphy, a great fierce Irish priest, declare that there was sure damnation for everyone outside the Church, I looked upon him with horror, and to that moment I trace the first rift which has grown into such a chasm between me and those who were my guides.

Though he did not become an atheist, he rejected most church doctrine and organized religion itself, continuing to search for religious answers compatible with his scientific and medical education. By the time he was writing *The Narrative of John Smith*, he had begun to experiment with psychic phenomena, a road that would culminate in his acceptance of spiritualism in 1916.

The themes in the *Narrative* had autobiographical sub-texts as well, instances of which are annotated in the text. Conan Doyle wanted readers to witness the high-mindedness of the physician's calling, even as he argued the incompleteness of medical knowledge, and inveighed against the smugness of the scientific establishment constantly enthroning its current set of theories as unquestionable fact. He not only praised Pasteur's new views on microbes and antibodies, he championed theories such as evolution that were very controversial at the time. Against occasional scientific opposition to such views, he saw even worse pomposity and bigotry in organized religion – finding truer religious feeling in a metaphysics of medicine than in the settled doctrines of the churches, and quoting dozens of thinkers against the latter. At one point Smith debates with a cleric calling upon him at home, outraging the latter into departing in high dudgeon, an episode that may be based upon an actual incident in Conan Doyle's early Southsea days.

Smith may be of middle age, but his opinions and the fervour with which he argues them are those of a young man with insufficient experience of life as yet to have become diffident regarding life, society, human nature and the like. Conan Doyle held some of those beliefs to the end of his life, but not all. In 1910, in a talk at St Mary's Hospital, London, entitled 'The Romance of Medicine,'[10] he looked back with greater humility at what he and his contemporaries at Edinburgh in the 1870s had believed about science as the answer to everything. In Chapter 5, when Smith turns to human nature again, he calls Woman but a 'supplement of a man.' If that was Conan Doyle's view then, it was not how he presented women in his later fiction. It also seems inconsistent with his view at the time of his mother, Mary Foley, who was better educated than most women in Victorian Britain, and had a strong personality and will of her own. After he had more experience under his belt, some of his later literary heroines were very independent women indeed.

One more major theme arises in Chapter 2 and continues to the end: Empire and Nations. Conan Doyle came to maturity in the heyday of the British Empire, and as a youth read much of the fiction of empire, such as G.A. Henty's novels, but this had not previously been a particular theme in his work. It is such here, often using the retired Major living upstairs as a foil. The tone of neither is jingoistic, even though the Major at one point is willing, even eager, to resort to force over a perhaps imaginary Russian offence in Asia. Not only Smith but also the Major describe in firm terms the human cost of war and the bureaucratic stupidities accompanying empire. Smith, described as having spent much of his life in the colonies, believes out there is where life is really life, at both its best and its worst. But Conan Doyle also looks into the far future to see the British Empire but third of the world's four great powers, outranked not only by the kindred United States but also by China. Even so, in Chapter 5, the last complete chapter in the novel, the final few pages are devoted to a poem very Kiplingesque in tone about colonial warfare, 'Corporal Dick's Promotion,' which Conan Doyle would include in other work of his in years ahead.

For all its energy and ideas, *The Narrative of John Smith* conspicuously lacks the storytelling technique that would distinguish Conan Doyle's later career. It affords a striking contrast with *The Stark Munro Letters*, written some ten years later, in which the author made use of many of the earlier manuscript's ideas and incidents, but with canny revisions demonstrating his growth as a writer. Dr Stark Munro is a young man struggling to find his way in the world, imparting an atmosphere of discovery to its long passages concerning ideas and philosophy. In the hands of the older, becalmed John Smith, these same passages had quickly descended into pedantry. 'You have degraded what should have been a course of lectures into a series of tales,' Sherlock Holmes once complained to Dr Watson, accusing himself of 'pandering to popular taste' in his accounts of the detective's cases. By that measure, Holmes might well have preferred *John Smith*, but most readers will gravitate to the Watsonian romanticism of *Stark Munro*.

Be that as it may, *The Narrative of John Smith* affords a rare glimpse of Conan Doyle's apprentice period, and demonstrates at least one attribute essential to any professional writer: he was not afraid to set aside a failing manuscript – nor to go back to it for elements he could usefully rework for later tales. Conan Doyle's later comments about the *Narrative* make it clear that he was well aware of the many shortcomings of this juvenile effort and, indeed, that he was embarrassed by it. In the same article in *The Idler* – again referring to the lost manuscript and perhaps offering a warning to future scholars and editors of his work – he wrote: 'I must in all honesty confess that my shock at its disappearance would be as nothing to my horror if it were suddenly to appear again – in print.'

Why, then, did he take the trouble to embark on rewriting a novel of which he had serious doubts at the time? However harsh his retrospective judgement might have been, and although he abandoned it – for reasons unknown – before he completed the rewriting, it seems likely that he at least began to reconstruct the text in the belief that it might yet be a work worth saving. Indeed, his dismissive comments about the work are not borne out by the fact that numerous similar and sometimes verbatim passages from it were retained in some subsequent works of his (including *The Stark Munro Letters*, *Through the Magic Door*, and some others noted in the annotations to the text).

Incomplete and in a state of arrested revision, the *Narrative* remained a work-in-progress for Conan Doyle. Although one which he eventually had second thoughts about publishing, it nonetheless has a significant part to play in allowing a fuller understanding of his development as a writer; and thus, we believe, offers ample justification for us to transgress his wishes and allow it to appear – in print.

their own turn comes round to be patients and then they raise up their voices and bellow with the best of us.

"A week's rest is essential to your cure"

"It's very hard" I grumbled "I am an open-air man, and have not spent a day indoors for five years. ~~of fun going on the height of the season, and I engaged ten deep. What could be more awkward!~~ Surely if I get well enough to walk without pain I may go out?"

"My dear Mr Smith" said Doctor Turner screwing up his stethoscope and picking up his very shiney broad-brimmed hat "If you wish to run the risk of pericarditis, endocarditis, embolism, thrombosis and metastatic abscess, you will go out. If not you will stay where you are"

As an argument it was a "clincher". I felt that nothing short of a conflagration or an earth-quake would move me off the sofa. The very names sent a pringling and a tingling through my system. "Not another word, Doctor," said I "I take my complaints one at a time. I am not a selfish man. Why should I have all these when there are so many poor folk who have not an ache to their backs. But for goodness' sake what am I to do with myself? I shall die of ennui"

"Not a bit of it" he answered cheerily with his hand upon the handle of the door "What is it the poet says? 'The mind is it's own place and in itself, can make a Hell of Heaven, a Heaven of Hell'. You must get your books round you and have a literary gorge to atone for your bodily abstinence. Or better still, get pen, ink and paper, and grind out something of your own. It has been said that every human being has within him the possibility of producing one good book. It's obviously untrue but all the same there may be some 'mute inglorious Miltons' about, who might have blossomed into poets or novelists had they been planted in proper soils.

"Depend upon it" said I sententiously "if

CHAPTER I

'GOUT OR RHEUMATISM, Doctor?' I asked.[1]

'A little of both, Mr Smith,' said he.

'And pray, sir, what is the exact difference between them?' I continued, under a natural impulse to gain a little knowledge in exchange for the red-hot skewer which was transfixing my right foot.

'Why,' said my good physician, tapping his tortoise-shell snuff box,[2] 'the one is a punishment and the other is a misfortune – one is in the hands of Providence and the other in your own. You can't command the weather which governs your rheumatism, but you can command your appetites which govern your gout.'

'And so,' said I, 'this diabolical pain in my foot is the hybrid form of torture known as rheumatic gout which unites the disadvantages of both diseases to a dash of malignancy all its own.'

'You are certainly suffering from rheumatic gout,' observed Dr Turner.

'And can only be cured by colchicum?'[3]

'And alkalis,' cried the doctor.

'And flannel?'

'And poppyheads,' cried the doctor.[4]

'And abstinence?'

'And a week's complete rest.'

'A week!' I roared, partly from emotion and, frankly, in response to a twinge which shot through my foot. 'Do you seriously imagine, Doctor, that I am going to lie upon this sofa for a week?'[5]

'Not a doubt of it,' he said composedly. It is astonishing how calm and free from all human weakness these doctors can be, until their own turn comes round to be patients and then they raise up their voices and bellow with the best of us. 'A week's rest is essential to your cure.'

'It's very hard,' I grumbled. 'I am an open-air man, and have not spent a day indoors for five years.⁶ Surely if I get well enough to walk without pain I may go out?'

'My dear Mr Smith,' said Dr Turner, screwing up his stethoscope and picking up his very shiny broad-brimmed hat. 'If you wish to run the risk of pericarditus, endo-carditus, embolism, thrombosis and metastatic abscess, you will go out. If not, you will stay where you are.'

As an argument it was a 'clincher.' I felt that nothing short of a conflagration or an earthquake would move me off the sofa. The very names sent a pringling and a tingling through my system. 'Not another word, Doctor,' said I. 'I take my complaints one at a time. I am not a selfish man. Why should I have all these when there are so many poor folk who have not an ache to their backs? But for goodness sake, what am I to do with myself? I shall die of ennui.'

'Not a bit of it,' he answered cheerily, with his hand upon the handle of the door. 'What is it the poet says? "The mind is its own place and in itself can make a hell of heaven, a heaven of hell."⁷ You must muster your books round you and have a literary gorge to atone for bodily abstinence. Or better still, get pen, ink and paper, and grind out something of your own. It has been said that every human being has within him the possibility of producing one good book. It is obviously untrue but all the same there may be some "mute inglorious Miltons"⁸ about, who might have blossomed into poets or novelists had they been planted in proper soils.'

'Depend upon it,' said I, sententiously, 'if man has a talent it will find its way out of him. The frost of poverty will never nip it entirely.'⁹

The Doctor let go of the handle and took a step back into the room, for he was a dogmatic little fellow, and as a natural consequence very intolerant of the dogmatism of others.

'No, but that of wealth will,' said he. 'The want of money is the sun which shines on the needy genius and warms his latent powers into life. I consider the possession of a competence to be one of the greatest curses which can befall a young man of talent.' He was so carried away by his subject that he took another step forward and plumped down into my easy chair. 'How many a promising lad I have known in my student days, who had it in him to rise to the highest honours of his profession. Yet the possession of a miserable hundred or two hundred a year has removed the chief incentive to work and caused him to dawdle along in an ignoble *dolce far niente*, while penniless youths with half his brains, driven by the sharp spur of necessity, passed over his head and soon bade fair to have a yearly income which equalled his capital. If it applies to medicine it does so even more to all that I know of literature. The best and most successful writers seem to find the undertaking of a new work to be a painful effort. Carlyle talks of returning to his writing "not like a warrior going to the battlefield, but like a slave lashed back to his task." If that is the feeling of an eminently successful man, how heavy and weary is the drudgery of the tyro who has no memories of former triumphs to bear him up. I tell you if a man is not *forced* to do it, he won't do it, unless indeed he is some *lusus naturae* like Macaulay,[10] who played with pens when he was in the nursery and preferred an ink pot to a Noah's ark. A man with brains and a competence may fail, but a man with brains and poverty must succeed.'

'So they said to Lord Southampton apropos of his son,' I observed. 'Do you remember his Lordship's reply? "If Providence," he said, "will find him the brains, I'll answer for the poverty."'[11]

Dr Turner had a good hearty laugh which was as invigorating as his most tonic prescription. 'He should have had the brains too with so witty a father,' he remarked. 'But I must positively hurry on. Look at this!' He showed a long column of names. 'They have all to be seen before I get home. Goodbye! Hope to find you better tomorrow. A little Irish whisky or a dry hock if you must have stimulants.' He closed the door behind him and was gone.

Now there's a man, thought I, as I listened to the dying rumble of his carriage wheels, who does an infinite amount of good in the world. Let me reduce it to figures. Supposing him to see forty patients a day – which is a moderate computation enough for a man in good practice – that would come to 14,600 a year.[12] And supposing him to be in active practice for thirty-five years, which again is a fair average, the total number of his visits and consultations would come to 511,000. Of these half million people the great majority, we will charitably suppose, have received benefits from his advice and prescriptions. What a colossal amount of good then will this one cheery unassuming mortal achieve before he finishes his career. Will his Grace of Canterbury do as much – or his Highness in the Vatican? 'Pon my word that square-edged professional hat should excite as much reverence as mitre or tiara, could we but look past the forms of things, and get at the things themselves.

There is the true function of the seer which St Thomas of Chelsea[13] preached so long and so earnestly. Blessings on his rugged shade, say I, wherever he may be! If ever a man realised the grand old type by walking straight and speaking fearlessly and practising himself what he preached to others it was surely the son of the stone mason of Ecclefechan. Of all sad literary episodes the attacks upon the great man's memory when the earth was still brown upon his grave were to my mind the most distressing. The jackals were silent enough while the old lion lived, but when he lay powerless and speechless there was none too small to have a snap or a pinch at him.

Oh these blow-flies of literature! What innate love of carrion is it which causes them ever to swarm upon the least healthy aspect of a great mind! Let a man have fifty of the noblest virtues and a single petty vice, straightaway the blow-fly critic comes along and settles upon that one failing and breeds such a spawn of pamphlets and articles that the casual reader can see no aspect of the man's character save the one least favourable one. Addison was a tenderhearted estimable man – 'but a drunkard' buzzes the blow-fly. Burns was generous and noble-minded – 'but a profligate!' buzzes the blow-fly. Coleridge has left us words which breathe the very spirit of virtue. 'Opium! Opium!' drones the blow-fly. Carlyle was a latter-day prophet. 'But look at his temper!' cry innumerable swarms of blow-flies.

His temper indeed! 'Anger is one of the sinews of the mind, and he who hath it not has a maimed soul,' says old Fuller.[14] Who ever did any good in the world without having some capabilities for righteous wrath within him? Do you suppose the Man from Nazareth was in the sweetest of tempers when he scourged the money lenders, or that his eyes did not flash and his colour heighten when he thundered out his Philippic against the Pharisees? Let us condone a little asperity in Carlyle then. A strong mind in a domestic circle is too often as overpowering as a loud instrument in a small chamber. It is not the instrument which is at fault but its environment. Who can read the exquisitely tender letters which passed between him and 'his little life partner,' when both were grey-headed, without feeling that their differences during forty years must have been small indeed to leave their love so fresh?

'One way or another all the light and energy and order and genuine *Thatkraft* or available virtue we have does come out of us and goes very infallibly into God's treasury, living and working through eternities there. We are not lost, not a solitary atom of us – of one of us.' There, my blow-fly, when you can evolve a sentence like that you may show a little temper too![15]

A week upon a sofa! When we see in the morning paper that some tramp has been condemned to seven days' hard labour for having no visible means of subsistence, or to fourteen for abstracting the said means from a baker's counter, it seems a small enough matter to us. How about the tramp, however! Seven nights of plank bed, seven dinners of skilly,[16] seven days of treadmill – the judge's sentence offers to him a long perspective of misery. Looking forward from this melancholy Monday morning, my week of seclusion stretches to formidable proportions. No doubt it will seem small indeed to look back upon. 'To those that enter,' says Plutarch, 'life seems infinite. To those that depart, nothing.' Looking back after an aeon or two to our mortal existence what an infinitesimal speck of a thing it will appear!

Yet I should be able to put in a week with a tolerable degree of comfort. As I pull myself up upon my sofa and take a good look round me I can find little fault with my surroundings. I have always, during a wandering, thriftless life, had an idea that I should like to find myself afloat in some snug little den in which I might duly enshrine my weather-beaten Lares and Penates. I had formed theories too of furnishing and of ornamentation which I have only now been able to put into practice. The choice of inanimate companions is to my mind only second to that of animate ones. Show me a man's chambers and I'll give you a pretty fair estimate of his intellect and capacity.[17] What the eye rests upon, the mind will dwell upon. It is easier to think daintily in a parlour than in an attic.

My sitting room is sixteen feet square – small enough for comfort and large enough for ample breathing space. Carpet, amber and black – none of your wishy-washy yellows, but a deep glowing lustrous amber, so that the two tiger skins upon it show up a shade or two lighter. Curtains to the broad bow window are of the same rich tint, and hang – not from a brazen abomination a foot or so deep – but from a thin square-edged gilt rod running round the whole apartment and serving to support the pictures as well. The walls are painted – not papered – the lightest seagreen, and the pictures in broad plain frames of dead gold lie *flat* against them, and not suspended at strange angles under the mistaken impression that they are rendered more visible thereby. The mantel-border corresponds in shade with the carpet and the white marble fireplace is paved with encaustic tiles which, though colourless themselves, will reflect a ruddy glow from the winter's fire. So much for the inside lining of my sanctum. Then, in furniture, I am still true to my amber and black.

Three straight-backed chairs in ebony frameworks and plush cushions are enough with two good *deep* armchairs of the same. A man, to get the full benefit of an armchair, should not sit on it but should rest upon his lower dorsal vertebrae. One broad comfortable sofa to which I am now confined. A sexagonal ebony table somewhere near the centre. Two smaller circular ones with

amber plush tops which you may move about at will and litter with
books and papers – or colchicum and liniments. No antimacassars!
One homely wicker-work chair, with padded seat and back, gives
an air of easy comfort and at the same time shows up the rest of
the furniture as a patch sets off a woman's complexion.

As to pottery, now that artistic vases are so cheap and so
beautiful there is no excuse for not having plenty of them. There
is one sound rule! In selecting them I eschew Dresden China
Shepherdesses or any other representation of animate beings. They
all smack of vulgarity. Pure symmetrical or geometrical designs
are more satisfying to the eye than any representation of natural
objects can be. Every variety of spheroid body, curving handle
and tapering neck is admissible, from the strictly classical to the
borders of the grotesque. I am not afraid of having too many rich
colours. Dame Nature mixes them all up on her great palette,
whether in the evening sky or in the summer meadows, and yet
no one has ever accused the good old lady of want of taste.

In the matter of pictures, one is enough for each side of the room,
but it should be a good one. The worst engraving of a first-class
composition is infinitely superior to a second-class original. The
subjects should be such as will inspire thought. Wilkie's 'Blind
Man's Buff' or 'Village Holiday' are pictures full of life and vigour,
but what earthly good is any man going to attain by a perpetual
contemplation of them? Here are two etchings by Doré, a print of
a dreamy allegorical picture of Noel Paton's, a study by William
Blake, and a fiery little engraving all bustle and life from one of
De Neuville's battle pieces.[18] They are all good of their sort and all
suggestive. Then I have a flat ebony mirror above the mantelpiece.
When a room is pretty, one need not fear to have it doubled.

And then the knick-knacks! Those are the things which give
the individuality to a room – the flotsam and jetsam which a
man picks up carelessly at first, but which soon drift into his
heart. If it conduces to comfort to have these little keepsakes of
the past before one's eyes, then what matter how inelegant they
may chance to be! When elegance and comfort clash, elegance
must go to the wall. Mr Boffin's philosophy was superior to that

of his spouse.[19] Elegance is simply comfort in its highest degree of
development. The instant that it ceases to be comfortable it loses
its whole *raison d'être*.

All these things which are littered about or stacked in corners
have a meaning in my eyes.[20] When the old leaky ship comes
lurching into port after her long voyage she bears with her whole
colonies of barnacles which have attached themselves to her
bottom. These things are the barnacles which cling on to me as a
visible sign of my wanderings. That is a Roman amphora dredged
up in the Bay of Baiae. Some gay old yachting party tumbled it
overboard at a time when the Roman quidnuncs[21] were gossiping
over Julius Caesar's descent upon the tin islands, and the men of
science were adding the village of Londinium to their maps of the
world. Here is an old blood-clotted scaling knife with which I have
removed a good many of the sealskin jackets which Nature, the
good old furrier, has provided for her Arctic children. Here is the
head too of a bear that I shot, and the ear-bone of a whale that I
helped to catch, and a necklace of cowrie shells that I purchased
from the young lady who wore it somewhere up the ill-omened
Bight of Benin. Here too are my Sierra Leone calabashes, and my
old boxing gloves with the horsehair all sticking out. As I look at
them a scene of thirty years ago stands out sharp and clear in my
memory. In a dim dusty room stands a square little man facing
a long thin one, like a flask of Hollands opposite a hock bottle.[22]
Each is drawing on a pair of boxing gloves, for the little man is
lightweight champion of Scotland and the other is a raw-boned,
loose-jointed student who is desirous of studying under so renowned
a professor.[23] Says the long man to himself, 'Now, I am heavier and
longer in the reach than this little fellow, and if I rush upon him
hitting with both hands I can hardly fail to bear him down.' It
was an enterprising thought and the last one that the novice had
for some little time, beyond a general impression that he had got
entangled in the machinery of an ocean liner which whirled him
here and whirled him there until a thousand horse-power piston
came smack between his eyes and he learned that it was a vulgar
error that stars cannot be seen in the daytime. 'That's what we

calls the postman's knock, sir,' said the champion blandly. 'You must try and not forget it.'[24] I never have. I find that it does not require much effort of memory.

By the way, all this digression upon furnishing and furniture is entirely involuntary and simply comes from my desire to make it clear that my week's imprisonment was less arduous than it might have been. The room was bright and its contents after my own heart. My income is moderate but I have made economy one of the exact sciences and I think that I extract the greatest possible amount of comfort from the money, and yet may have a few pounds over at the year's end to help any poor devil who is less lucky than myself. I confess to one little extravagance – and only one. You see those four squat oak cases, their well-stocked shelves lined with rich brown leather stamped with gold. Those books are the collection of a lifetime. Run your eye over them. Petrarch, Ruskin, Boswell, Goethe, Tourguenieff, Richter, Emerson, Heine, Darwin, Winwood Reade, Tertullian, Balzac – truly an august and cosmopolitan company.[25]

There should be a Society for the Prevention of Cruelty to Books. I hate to see the poor patient things knocked about and disfigured. A book is a mummified soul embalmed in morocco leather and printer's ink instead of cerecloths and unguents. It is the concentrated essence of a man. Poor Horatius Flaccus[26] has turned to an impalpable powder by this time, but there is his very spirit stuck like a fly in amber, in that brown-backed volume in the corner. A line of books should make a man subdued and reverent. If he cannot learn to treat them with becoming decency he should be forced.

If a bibliophile House of Commons were to pass a 'Bill for the better preservation of books' we should have paragraphs of this sort under the headings of 'Police Intelligence' in the newspapers of the year 2000: 'Marylebone Police Court.[27] Brutal outrage upon an Elzevir Virgil. James Brown, a savage-looking elderly man, was charged with a cowardly attack upon a copy of Virgil's poems issued by the Elzevir press. Police Constable Jones deposed that on Tuesday evening about seven o'clock some of the neighbours complained to him of the prisoner's conduct. He saw him sitting at an open window with the book in front of him which he was dog-earing, thumb-marking and otherwise ill using. Prisoner expressed the greatest surprise upon being arrested. John Robinson, librarian of the casualty section of the British Museum, deposed to the book, having been brought in in a condition which could only have arisen from extreme violence. It was dog-eared in thirty-one places, page forty-six was suffering from a clean cut four inches long, and the whole volume was a mass of pencil – and finger – marks. Prisoner, on being asked for his defence, remarked that the book was his own and that he might do what he liked with it. Magistrate: "Nothing of the kind, sir! Your wife and children are your own but the law does not allow you to ill treat them! I shall decree a judicial separation between the Virgil and yourself, and condemn you to a week's hard labour." Prisoner was removed, protesting. The book is doing well and will soon be able to quit the museum.'

What a wonderful, wonderful thing it is, though use has dulled our admiration of it! Here are all these dead men lurking inside my oaken case, ready to come out and talk to me whenever I may desire it. Do I wish philosophy? Here are Aristotle, Plato, Bacon, Kant and Descartes, all ready to confide to one their very inmost thoughts upon a subject which they have made their own. Am I dreamy and poetical? Out come Heine and Shelley and Goethe and Keats with all their wealth of harmony and imagination. Or am I in need of amusement on the long winter evenings? You have but to light your reading lamp and beckon to any one of the world's great storytellers, and the dead man will come forth and prattle to you by the hour. That reading-lamp is the real Aladdin's wonder for summoning the genii with. Indeed, the dead are such good company that one is apt to think too little of the living.

[surviving portion of a passage cut out of the manuscript] crystals and hideous accompaniments, are infinitely softer and more pleasant to the eye. I can understand a lunatic asylum managed on home rule principles preferring the gas-flare, but how the general public has come to adopt it passes my understanding.[28]

I can imagine that when an Antipodean or African scientist about the year of grace 7000 begins to make excavations and researches among the mounds which mark the former situation of London, nothing which he unearths will puzzle him more than the gas-pipes. By that time all memory of the vile compound will have left this planet – its place having been taken by the successor to the successor to the electric light. Drainpipes and water pipes will be within the savant's range of comprehension, but in Heaven's name what are these miles and miles of corroded narrow-gauged tubing![29] This is something like the report which will appear in the New Guinea Quarterly Review of the learned disquisition by the Doctor Dryasdust of the period.

'At the third annual meeting of the New Guinea Archaeological Society a paper was read by Dr Dryasdust F.N.G.A.S. upon recent researches on the supposed site of London, together with some observations upon hollow cylinders in use among the Londoners. Several examples of these cylinders or tubings were on exhibition in the hall and were passed round for inspection among the audience. The learned lecturer prefaced his remarks by observing that on account of the enormous interval of time which separated them from the days when London was a flourishing city, it behooved them to weigh the evidence very carefully before coming to any definite conclusions as to the habits of the inhabitants. There appeared to be no doubt that the date of the Fall of London was somewhat later than that of the erection of the Egyptian pyramids. A large building had recently been unearthed near the dried-up bed of the River Thames, and there could be no question from existing records that this was the seat of the law-making council among the Ancient Britons, or Anglicans as they are sometimes termed. Near this was a square brick building called the Aquarium, and serving, as the name implies, as a place of seclusion for habitual drunkards.[30] The lecturer proceeded to remark that there are strong reasons for believing that the city was at that time situated upon the seashore, since, as Professor Fungus has pointed out, one of the principal thoroughfares was known as the Strand. The bed of the Thames had been tunnelled under by a

monarch named Brunel who is supposed by some historians to have
succeeded Alfred the Great. The principal places of amusement
were Kensington (from the German root "kennen – to know," so
called with reference to certain schools of fine art and cookery)
– and Hyde Park, the name of which appeared to Dr Dryasdust
to suggest the possibility of treasures being concealed in it. These
open spaces must, however, have been far from safe, as the bones
of tigers, lions, and other large Carnivora have been discovered in
the adjoining Regent's Park. The lecturer, having briefly referred
to the mysterious structures known as "pillar-boxes", which are
scattered thickly over the city and which, he remarked, must be
regarded either as religious in their origin, or else as marking the
tombs of Anglican chiefs, passed on to the cylindrical piping. This
had been described by Dr Fungus as having formed a complex and
universal system of lightning conductors. He (the lecturer) could
not assent to his theory. In a series of observations extending over
several years he had discovered the important fact that these lines
of tubing, if followed out, invariably led to large hollow metallic
chambers which were connected with furnaces. No one who knew
how addicted the Ancient Britons were to tobacco could doubt what
this meant. Evidently, large quantities of this herb were burned in
the central reservoir and the aromatic and narcotic vapour was
carried through the tubes to the house of every citizen so that he
might inhale it at will. Having illustrated his theory by a series
of diagrams, the lecturer concluded by remarking that modern
science had thrown such a light upon Old London that, from the
moment of the citizen taking his tub or tab in the morning[31] until
after a draught of porter he painted himself blue before retiring
to rest, every action of his life was known.'

I daresay there is as much foundation for most of the above as
for Piazzi Smyth's Theory of the Great Pyramid,[32] or our ideas of
life among the Babylonians. It's best not to be dogmatic on those
matters. But I must really drop these [narrative cuts off]

This room of mine which I have described with such prolixity
is a second-floor front in a quiet London thoroughfare. The wave
of fashion passed over this quarter a century or so ago and has

left a deposit of eminent respectability behind it. You can see the long iron extinguishers upon the railings where the link-boys used to put out their torches, instead of banging them about on the pavement or stamping upon them as was the custom in less high-toned neighbourhoods. There are the high curb-stones too, so that Lady Teazle or Mrs Sneerwell could step out of coach or sedan chair without soiling their dainty satin shoes.[33] Dear me, what a very unstable chemical compound man is, to be sure! Here are all the little stage accessories still standing while the players have all split up into hydrogen and oxygen and nitrogen and carbon, with traces of iron and silica and phosphorus and a few other ingredients. Look at this picture and on that! High-born bucks of the period, mincing ladies, swaggering bullies, scheming courtiers – see how they are planning and pushing and striving each to attain his own petty object! Now for a jump of seventy years – good heavens, what is this! Margarine and cholesterine, carbonates and sulphates, ptomaines and liquescence – yet that nauseous mass is human life reduced to its least common denominator.

And yet I have a very high respect for the human body and I hold that it has been unduly snubbed and maligned by divines and theologians. 'Our gross frames' and 'our miserable mortal clay' are phrases which to my mind partake more of blasphemy than of piety. It is no compliment to the Creator to depreciate His handiwork. Whatever theory or belief we may hold about the soul, there can be no question that the body is immortal. Matter may be transformed from one shape to another but it can never be destroyed. If a comet were to strike this dust-heap of ours and to knock it into a billion fragments which flew right and left into space, if its fiery breath were to lick up every living form as a moth is shrivelled up in a candle; still, at the end of a thousand million years, every tiniest particle of our bodies would still exist – in other forms and combinations it is true – but still the very identical molecules which we now bear about in our organisation. Not a nucleolus would be wanting. How far we may impress our own individuality upon the ultimate atoms of our composition is a question which will bear a very considerable amount of discussion.[34] The facts of embryology may be taken to indicate that every tiny organic cell of which a man is composed contains in its microcosm a complete miniature of the individual of which it forms a part. The ovum itself from which we are all produced is less than one two-hundredth part of an inch in diameter and yet within those narrow limits lies potentiality not only for reproducing the features of two individuals, but even their smallest tricks of habit or thought.

There is reason to believe that every microscopic cell, billions of which go to make up a human unit, has the latent power within it of developing under certain conditions an entire individual. Have you ever heard of dermoid cysts? They are among the most mysterious of pathological conditions. A man perceives a lump to be forming on his eyebrow, or his shoulder, or any other part of his person. It increases rapidly until it attains alarming proportions. He hurries to a surgeon who, under the impression that the swelling is an abscess, opens it and finds – teeth, hair, bones, perhaps even some attempt at the formation of an arm or a leg. These cases are by no means uncommon in the annals of surgery. Apparently nothing but the defective blood supply of the part has prevented the formation of a perfect human being. What are we to understand by that? So startling a phenomenon must have some deep meaning. I imagine that the true explanation is that every cell in our organisations has a power latent in it by which it may reproduce the whole individual, and that occasionally under some special circumstances – some obscure local nervous or vascular excitement – one of these microscopic units of structure actually does make a clumsy attempt in that direction.

But, dear me, what very deep waters we have got ourselves into! All this comes from my endeavouring to show that it was within the bounds of possibility that the ultimate atoms of our composition – which are to all appearance immortal – may bear to the end of time some impress of our individuality. John's dust may always retain something of John about it and be eternally distinguishable from that of Tom. The moral of which is that since our bodily constituents will have work of one sort or another to do for countless ages it is our duty to cultivate them and keep them in the highest state of efficiency. Train lads' minds by all means, but don't neglect their bodies. I hate the bulbous-headed bicep-less youth who knows everything and does nothing. He is not the highest expression of modern civilisation any more than an encyclopaedia is the crowning glory of literature.[35] Give me a lad who has good warm blood in his veins, who can do the mile in 5.30 or throw a cricket ball a hundred yards, and I'll forgive some little ignorance as to Greek roots or the formation of the second aorist in irregular verbs. His bright eye and brown cheek bespeak a power of acting which will probably be of more value to the community at large than his white-faced companion's power of accumulating knowledge. It is only when you have the two powers largely developed in the same individual that you get a very superior type of man – a Newton, a Stanley or a Lesseps.

Thought when reduced to practice is the mainspring of the world, but I fancy we are inclined to attach too much importance to it in the abstract. The fifty moral philosophers who have come to fifty different conclusions about the nature of the will may have all been very estimable gentlemen, but they have not advanced the weal of the human race in any appreciable degree, and that, after all, is the touchstone on which the value of a man's life's labour should be tested. Take the case of a navvy who has had a hand in the digging of the Suez Canal. That man has undoubtedly contributed during his lifetime to the carrying out of a project which has benefited the world, and we are all therefore so much the better for his existence. But how about Kant of Königsberg? If he and his theories had never been heard of, what would we be the worse? I fancy the navvy has rather the best of the comparison.

Mrs Rundle my landlady has just been up to enquire about my foot. She is a buxom, timorous woman with her heart full of kindness and her head of devices for making both ends meet. I need hardly remark that she is a widow. During a long and varied experience of lodgings I had become so accustomed to having widows as landladies that the two ideas were synonymous in my mind.[36] On a recent occasion, however, shortly after entering into new apartments, I perceived a little cross-eyed red-bearded man crawling about the staircase whom I promptly arrested as a suspicious character. To my astonishment he claimed to be the landlady's husband, and his assertion was borne out by the matron herself and by the servant girl, so it seems there is no rule without an exception.

Mrs Rundle has seen better times but is now in reduced circumstances. Lodging-house keepers are like the price of land, forever reduced and never to rise. Her husband used to be 'in the City,' which is an elastic term meaning anything from a commissionaire to a bank-director. She has three children, poor soul, and a hard fight to bring them up to her own satisfaction. At nine-thirty sharp I see them trotting off to school with a perfect polish upon their chubby faces from vigorous washing, and at four or thereabouts they return in such a mess that they leave a dinginess in the very air as they pass through it. If the learning they acquire is in any proportion to the dirt they must be three little Solomons.

At present matters must, I should judge, be going well with the Rundle family. They themselves occupy the basement of the house, which is mysteriously divided into their apartments and those of two domestics. On the ground floor is a very eligible tenant, Herr Johann Lehmann, Professor of Music, who growls on his grand piano or screams on his violin from early in the morning till late at night. The Herr Professor is a permanent lodger and a good one – I daresay he represents three guineas a week, for I pay two upon the floor above. Then on the top floor of all there dwells an ancient half-pay officer[37] who appears to be quiet and inoffensive in his ways, though I hear that he has been known once or twice about quarter-day to be a little merry and to sing old-fashioned songs in a high cracked voice at untimely hours. Putting the veteran's contribution at a guinea we arrive at the respectable sum of six guineas a week as Mrs Rundle's income. On the other hand, she contends that rent and taxes are enormous, servants' wages ruinous, and meat at a shilling a pound – so perhaps there is no very great margin after all.

A wandering life is apt to take the finer edge off a man's soul. Contact with women and children develops the more amiable virtues. When a man has drifted about for thirty years over half the known world, and has never remained under one roof for six months at a time it rubs some of the varnish off him and tries his character as well as his constitution. Now I have been a rolling stone all my life and what is worse I am conscious that I have been a failure. As a boy at college, as a student at Edinburgh, as a literary man in London, as a soldier in America, as a traveller in many lands, as a diamond digger at the Cape, [38] I have always had the same sense of failure. 'But look how successful you have been!' cry my friends. It is true that I have amassed enough to satisfy my wants and to secure my old age, but is that success? Ah, if I had my time over again how very much better I could do it all!

Literature is a very tempting oyster for a smart young man to open, but your knife is apt to break short off before you get into it.[39] Oh you brilliant and coruscating ones, who sail through the firmament of letters with all the magazines fighting for the sparks which you emit, how can you realise how dreary a profession it is to your less gifted brethren? If the secret history of literature could be written, the blighted hopes, the heart-sickening disappointments, the weary waiting, the wasted labour, it would be the saddest record ever penned. Have I not known the genius of the family, boy or girl, buckle to bravely produce a maiden romance, which should take the public by storm and relieve the weight of liabilities which were pressing the old folk down? Very slowly and very laboriously, with much knitting of brows and burning of oil, chapter is added to chapter. Soon the book takes substance and form. Extracts are read from it to the assembled family and are hailed with laughter and tears by every member, from the six-year-old to the doddering grandfather who claps his thin hands together with delight. Never was such a novel written – never! Who ever heard of so villainous a villain, or of so heroic a hero? Flushed and proud the coming author pushes on with redoubled vigour until some fine day he writes a great FINIS at the end of the third volume and springs from his seat in triumph, while his good mother conceals the pen in her private drawer of valuables, as being an article which will one day be regarded as a relic. Now who shall have the honour of publishing it? Oh, the best of course. Brown, Jones and Robinson are a high-toned firm. They are the very men to bring out such a work. Off it goes to London, duly packed, addressed, and registered, with every conceivable precaution against its miscarrying.[10] A month passes pleasantly enough while the family discuss what is to be done with the proceeds of the book. There is Freddy's education to be thought of,[11] and the getting of the Genius himself into a profession unless he determines to confine himself to literature. It is all arranged and rearranged. The second month comes and there is a hurry down in the morning and a pricking of ears for the postman's step – but still no letter from London. Another month passes. 'Perhaps we had better write and enquire,' the father suggests timidly. 'No, no,' says the Genius, 'it always takes some time for them to arrange the getting out of a work of importance.' Two more months pass and at last the letter is written. What is this great roll upon the breakfast table with the London postmark? 'The book, father, the book!' cry brothers and sisters. The Genius unties it with trembling fingers, tears the brown paper open and reveals his manuscript all tattered and torn. Here is a little pencil note. 'B.J. and R. present their compliments to Mr – and regret that they have detained his M.S. so long. The delay arose from its having been mislaid. B.J. and R. regret to state that after careful perusal of the M.S. they are of opinion that it is entirely unfit for publication.' 'Never mind – we'll get it in somewhere,' cries the Genius in a crackling voice, feeling in a moment as if his heart had turned to a lump of lead. 'Of course we will,' says the father with a forced laugh. 'Then I'm not to go to school,' cries the little six-year-old. 'It will make a hit yet,' says the mother, gathering up the worthless roll of paper from the table. Ah, dear, it seems so strange and hard to them, and yet no post ever goes out of London which does not contain such another bundle and cause such another pang.

When I was a young fellow endeavouring to earn bread and cheese with my pen – a halfpenny worth of cheese to an intolerable amount of bread – I always had some hope to cheer me and some second string to my bow on which to depend if the first should snap. In that, I was of course more fortunate than many another poor devil who was toiling along the same narrow and thorny track. I had, however, my fair share of rebuffs and disappointments. The articles which I sent forth came back to me at times with a rapidity and accuracy which spoke well for our postal arrangements. If they had been paper boomerangs they could not have returned more infallibly to their unhappy dispatcher. There was one stale little cylinder of manuscript which described irregular orbits among the publishers until I became so weary of its perpetual reappearance that I consigned it to the flames. I am sore now, after a quarter of a century, when I think of it.[42] Ah, these children of our mind – the strong and robust can look after themselves, but our heart turns towards the weakly and deformed! An author has always a pride in his successful work, but it is as nothing compared with his love and pity for his failures.

But there was a brighter side to my own brief experiences. Occasionally, articles – even among the first which I evolved – went off without a hitch and made their appearance amidst the most august and select of company. Kindly letters from editors with allusions to enclosures made amends for many a failure. There was one gentleman, whose eminent position in the literary world must have made his time particularly valuable, but who managed to spare a few minutes in advising or exhorting the newest of novices. He superintended the whole garden of literature and the most unpromising and unattractive of plants might hope for some pruning and watering at his hands. I never received one of his brief and frequently illegible notes without a feeling of wonder and gratitude at the kindliness which prompted it.[43]

I fancy that since Walter Scott's famous dictum anent the staff and the crutch,[44] and Charles Lamb's still more pronounced opinion, there has been less inclination to take up literature as a profession. There is, I hope, no class now like the old gar-reteers in Grub Street, who must either write or starve.[45] Unless a man has met with such success in literature as to assure him of a comfortable income he rarely looks to it entirely for his subsistence. I know of no man who is placed in so sad a position as he who is gifted with an amount of literary ability which is just short of the standard demanded by the caterers for the public. An irresistible impulse drives him to write – an impulse which failure can never entirely overcome. His whole life is a toiling and a slaving to get within that magic circle – and dreary heartbreaking work it is.

Here are the three little Rundles coming home from school. I can see down the street from where I lie, thanks to the bow window. Dicky, Tommy and Maude are their names, of which if I remember right Dicky is the dirtiest and Tommy is the stickiest, while the little girl is chiefly remarkable for negative qualities. Hullo, some sort of a civil war has broken out among them! Dicky possesses something – toffee as I guess – which the other two are endeavouring to take away from him. Dicky fights gallantly but the allies are too strong for him. They bear away the plunder, but Tommy in the hour of victory refuses to share with Maude, so she relapses into tears and reproaches. What an epitome of all the wars and coalitions of history! And about as important perhaps in the eyes of omnipotence.

I learn the cause of the quarrel from Mrs Rundle when she comes up to lay my cloth. The problem as submitted by the belligerent powers is certainly a knotty one, which explains if it does not justify the recent outbreak of hostilities. A penny, and not toffee, had been the *casus belli*. The said penny had lain in the roadway as they returned from school and all three had spied it at the same time. Dicky, however, by dint of superior speed, had reached it first and had appropriated it. The other two made a claim for equal shares on the grounds that they were co-discoverers. On a refusal from the greedy Dicky the joint powers sent a combined ultimatum and eventually a declaration of war. The question is too complex a one for me to adjudicate upon, beyond remarking that Tommy's ultimate action was entirely indefensible. The fruit of this decision of mine became speedily apparent in a sound as of enthusiastic applause in the basement floor, followed by fearful

howls and the slamming of a door, from which I surmise that
Master Tommy has been dispatched to bed.

Do you know what the meaning of that phenomenon is which
some good people call 'inherent wickedness' and others 'original
sin'? Why is it that the child of four is apt to strike the child of
three – or that the capture and ill usage of some little insect or
animal is a sport which never palls upon the average infant? It
is a painful thought that the young human being takes to cruelty
as a young duck takes to water, until precept and punishment
teaches it to control its impulses and gradually eradicates them.
It arises, I think, from the hundred thousand years of barbarism
which our race has gone through. Every squall-faced bald-headed
baby is the lineal descendant of countless generations of savages
and the heir to all their instincts and peculiarities. Remember
that the era of civilisation is but the narrow golden border which
trims the dense blackness of primeval history. Left to its own
impulses the child would certainly revert to the type which is as
inherent to it as the number of its limbs or the mechanism of its
respiration. As reason dawns upon it, however, Christianity and
civilisation are forcibly grafted upon it just as a calf's lymph is
injected into its arm. Elevation of the mind and vaccination of
the body are equally artificial processes. If a nineteenth-century
child were left entirely to its own devices upon a desolate island it
would develop into a being who would be no whit better, either in
morality or in knowledge, than its Euskarian ancestor who lived
in a blue-lias cave and ground flints for arrowheads many many
thousands of years ago.

Courage though! There will come a time when the virtuous
instincts will gain the upper hand of the vicious ones. It will be
long – very long – in coming, but its advent is as certain as that
drops of acid falling constantly into an alkaline solution will
eventually precipitate a salt. When aeons of light and progress
have cancelled the effect of aeons of darkness and crime, then
our offspring will inevitably be born with a strong natural bias
towards all that is high and noble. In those happy days a child if
abandoned and untaught would from its own innate and hereditary

instincts lead a merciful, cleanly and innocent existence. Such a child would avoid evil, as a kitten avoids puddles, not from any personal or acquired knowledge of it, but from an ingrained and overpowering impulse. When infants do what is right without being told, and would rather help an insect on its way than pull its leg off, the millennium is not very far off.

This Education Act of ours is a wonderful measure, though still no doubt capable of improvement.[16] The coming Englishman looking back at nineteenth-century legislation will be astonished at its thorough provisions and admirable administration. Indeed I think we have hardly realised yet what its full effect will be upon the next generation. Competition is keen enough now — heaven knows — in every art and profession. If a man advertises for a clerk the street traffic is blocked with the applicants. What will it be then? Fifty per cent of the children may settle down into whatever their fathers were before them, but the other fifty with all this unwanted knowledge seething in their brains are not going to devote their lives to clipping hedges or digging drains. Ambition will lead them to crowd into what is already overcrowded with, I fear, disastrous results. The educated workman is excellent in theory but too often the workman ceases when the education begins. Still, however much individuals may suffer, what raises the standard of intelligence in a country must raise the country itself. The best educated country will eventually prove to be the strongest, and the welfare of the individuals makes the welfare of the community.

Ah me, it is colchicum time again, so I had best drop platitudes and look after realities. 'Write something!' says Doctor Turner, but how am I to write anything worth reading while my ankle is burning and starting? However, tomorrow if all is well I shall get out foolscap and goose-quill and make an effort. If I can be so garrulous in these wandering incoherent notes there should be some capacity for work in me yet. There's nothing I hate so much as idleness – except perhaps labour.

CHAPTER 2

'YOU ARE ABSOLUTELY SATURATED with lithic acid,'[47] said Dr Turner gravely. 'Your blood is in a most impure condition.'

'Then you think I am worse?'

'I think you are no better,' he answered. 'You must take great care of yourself or you will be in for a really serious attack. What is that little red spot on your wrist?'

'Nothing of any importance,' I replied.

'Humph!' said he. Some doctors can compress a good deal into that monosyllable. 'There's a good deal of fever about.'

The conversation began to get depressing. 'Talking of fevers,' I said, 'I have just been glancing over Monsieur Pasteur's researches on splenic fever in cattle. Don't you think they open up a great field of possibilities?'[48]

I had evidently hit upon a congenial topic. My physician laid down his hat and squared his elbows with his ten finger-tips in contact as was his habit when he intended to lay down the law. 'My dear sir,' said he, 'the happy issue of that series of experiments promises in time to revolutionise our medical practice and to make the healing art one of the exact sciences. It is a subject in which I take a deep professional interest and I am pleased to find that you, who have no direct interest in the matter, should have been turning your thoughts in that direction.'

'I am a dabbler in many things,' I remarked. 'Besides, I consider that every man has a direct interest in knowing what steps are being taken to stamp out disease.'

'Why, so they have,' the doctor answered, 'but our scientists use so many technicalities that it is not always easy for the uninitiated to follow them. "The inoculation of sterilized and attenuated virus caused inhibition of the vaso-motor centres and a modified cachexia tending towards peripheral and centripetal paralysis."[49] What layman is going to ruin his brain-digestion by taking such a tough morsel as that into it? In this matter of splenic fever the facts are, however, simple enough when denuded of polysyllables. Devaine in 1850 discovered the little rod-like body in the blood of the diseased cattle – "bacterium anthracis" he called it – and Koch of Wollstein proved that it would increase and multiply in chicken broth or any other nourishing medium just as well as in the animal's circulation. Then Pasteur took the matter up and showed that if bred in this artificial manner the little organisms, after prolonged exposure to the atmosphere, lose all their malignancy and can be injected into the veins of a bullock without producing more than a slight constitutional disturbance. And now comes the all-important practical conclusion. It was discovered that the cattle which had been treated with this weak solution of germs – or "inoculated by attenuated virus," to use the jargon of science – were rendered incapable of ever taking the original disease.'

'The cattle should be eternally grateful to Monsieur Pasteur,' I remarked.

'Not more than we should,' cried Dr Turner warmly. 'What applies to splenic fever among beasts will apply equally to every infectious disease which afflicts the human frame. They depend, each and all of them, upon the presence in the blood of these minute creatures, and their varying symptoms are due to the different malignancy of the microbes, or to their preference for this or that part of the body.[50] In time we shall have the attenuated virus of every one of these diseases, and by mixing them together will be able, by a single inoculation, to fortify the constitution against them. Zymotic disease, sir, will be stamped out. Typhus, typhoid, cholera, malaria, hydrophobia, scarlatina, diphtheria, measles and probably consumption will cease to exist – and all owing to the labours of Louis Pasteur – God bless him!'

'Why, Doctor,' said I, 'you are quite an enthusiast.'

'Yes,' he answered, mopping his flushed face. 'It's a subject which warms my very heart. We are at war with these pestilential atoms and when we gain a victory over them the whole human race should light up their candles and sing "Te Deum."[51] The most bloodthirsty tiger that ever trod a jungle is harmless compared to these microscopic spores and filaments, but the time is coming when they too will be forced to own man as the Lord of Creation. I'll show you some of them if you can come round to my laboratory when you are able to get about. I have Koch's bacillus of phthisis,[52] and the comma-shaped bacterium of cholera, and a score more of the little villains. I'm sure you would like to have a look at them.'

I'm sure I would rather keep at a distance from them, said I to myself as the good man took his departure. I wouldn't have such a collection in my house for anything I could name. I'm not more nervous than my neighbours about what I can see, but to run a chance of breathing in the concentrated essence of disease and of having one's blood choked up with fungoid growths is a little too much. I shall certainly keep clear of the doctor's laboratory.

It's one of the most praiseworthy and admirable things I know, the way in which the faculty are continually endeavouring to promote sanitary improvements and to stamp out disease *ab initio*. If they were not a most disinterested and high-minded body of men they would let things take their course, and content themselves with reaping the harvest. Who ever heard of a congress of lawyers for the purpose of simplifying the law and discouraging litigation? Unhealthy times mean good times for the medics. If they were to follow no higher dictates than those of their own interests, we should have the British Medical Association setting a fund on foot for the impeding of drainage and stopping up of sewers, while the General Council busied itself in the importation of epidemics and the distribution of germs. Of the 30,000 physicians and surgeons in the British Islands, the vast majority are practical philanthropists of the highest order. There, if that paragraph does not put the doctor in a good humour tomorrow, it won't be for want of showing it to him.

Mrs Rundle appeared after breakfast this morning with a colossal mustard poultice in which she wished to envelop my ankle. Strange how that tendency to fly to mustard as a remedy pervades the whole female sex. If you are suffering from anything, from a hiccough to hydrophobia, the average man recommends a drop of brandy and the average woman reaches for the mustard pot. On this occasion by a judicious mixture of argument and authority I succeeded in inducing her to remove the abomination, but I can see that she looks upon me as one who has had salvation offered him but has refused it. As a matter of fact my ankle is somewhat easier today, but I have an occasional gnawing at my wrist which I fear means mischief.

It is astonishing how seldom a sick man, be he where he may, meets with anything but kindness. There are more Good Samaritans than Levites in the world. I have been knocked over with malarial fever at Panama, with ague at Kimberley and with typhoid at a Monaco boarding house, but on each occasion I found some good-hearted Christian to give me a helping hand. I think it is Ruskin who remarks that if the Samaritan had been an Englishman he would have said, 'Two pence I leave with you – and I shall expect four pence when I come again this way.' I am very sure that my nurses were disinterested enough, for in those days the most sanguine of mankind would never have looked for anything at my hands.

Can I not see one of them now? Conkey Bill of Winter Rush, better known as the Cock of the Mines, square-shouldered and bearded, with a face as red as his shirt and a hand like a leg of mutton! Charity is a strange plant and sprouts in unlikely places, but I have ever found that the stoutest heart is inclined to be the softest. See him with the tiny phial between his great fingers endeavouring to measure the due allowance of fever drops and pattering to himself some devil's litany the while, for he always showed great freedom and finish in the use of adjectives. Or see the gleam of his white teeth and the broad smile of hearty delight when first I sat up on my couch and asked for food. Ah, Dick, my old pard, when you were shot in an obscure frontier skirmish, and buried like a dog on the banks of the Tugela, there was a seed planted which may sprout into an angel some day.[53]

Who says the human race is vicious, degenerate and biased towards evil? I do not envy the man who can say that he has found them so. He has either been most unfortunate in his associates, or he has viewed them with a jaundiced eye. It is true that, as I remarked yesterday, the infant has a tendency to relapse into savagery, but taking the adults of our acquaintance of either sex, where is this vileness of which we hear so much? Do we find the audience at the playhouse cheering the villain out of their sympathy with vice, or is the area-thief or wife-beater a popular character among the lower orders on the grounds of community of instincts? To hear some of our black-coated friends talk, one would think that if it were not for themselves and their sermons the citizens would become fiends and the state a pandemonium. 'Look at the police news!' they cry. Ah, but look at the lifeboat rescues, look at the annals of the Humane Society's medals and of the Albert medals, look at the devotion of nurses, look at that young doctor the other day, sucking the diptheritic membrane from a patient's throat and so catching the fatal malady. Is all this to go for nothing? There is seldom a fire that some brave man does not struggle through smoke and flame in search of human lives, seldom a man overboard that two do not spring to the rescue, never a mining accident that scores are not ready to face the deadly after-damp in the hope of lending aid to their companions. This is healthier reading than the police reports. Believe me, if the vice and the virtue of this world were thrown into the scales, the former would kick the beam.

But I will go a great deal further than this. I contend that a fair percentage of the population have attained such a point that they are within measurable distance of perfection. Among educated men, and far more among educated women, perfection or something very closely resembling it, is the normal condition.[34] Nay, never turn up your aquiline nose, my dear young cleric, or shake a dissentient head. I have seen more of this world of ours than you have, and perhaps with less prejudiced eyes. When Nature gave me a maternal pat on the head upon my fiftieth birthday, and knocked some of the pigment out of my hair, she gave me the right to be a little dogmatic about matters of experience. Perhaps now I might convince you in spite of yourself that I am right in this matter of perfection. Here, sir, is a clear sheet of foolscap and a pencil. Kindly take a seat in front of it. Now cast your mind back to your dear old mother, who strove so long and worked so hard to find the means for your education. Recall every incident which you can recollect of her life. Since human nature is so frail, and you have known her so intimately, you are best able to speak as to her frailties. Kindly write down a list upon that slip of paper of the principal faults which you have observed in her. What, at fault already! Nay, then, let us try another. Those two excellent and charitable young ladies, your sisters – perhaps you can jot down the main points which you would like to see reformed in their characters. You seem puzzled again. Then there is that other young lady whom you know pretty well – well, well – it would be flat blasphemy to set about reforming *her*.[55]

'It is true,' says our young theologian, 'that my mother and my sisters—'

'And somebody else's sister,' I interpolate.

'That they are all such favourable specimens of their sex that it would be difficult to suggest how their conduct or way of living could be improved, but that does not justify us in formulating such a proposition as the one you have put forward.'

'You must remember,' I answer, 'that I only made my claim for a percentage of the human race. Since your own relations are close to perfection, may not those of other people be so likewise.'

'They may seem perfect in the eyes of man,' said he, 'but it will be far otherwise in the sight of God.'

'If critical, carping man can find no fault in them,' I replied, 'they have not much to fear from an all-merciful Creator.'

The human race is improving – and improving rapidly. There is not one criminal conviction now for ten in the days of our grand-fathers. The uneducated classes have, for the most part, supplied our malefactors and when there cease to be any uneducated classes we may expect a great drop in our charge-lists. Here are some duly-attested figures which should warm your blood like cordial:

	Criminal convictions	Attendance at school
1868	17,394	1,150,000
1884	12,564	3,700,000

Thóse numbers should be printed up in letters of gold in every room in the kingdom, that a man may cheer his heart, when he is down, by glancing at them. I assure you that often when I see some brutal-looking fellow in the streets, with evil and ignorance – the devil's hallmarks – stamped upon his countenance, I stand and gaze at him with the utmost interest and curiosity. 'That fellow and his type,' I think to myself, 'will soon be as extinct as the Great Auk or the Dodo. Our children's children will never see anything approaching him.' I am not sure that we should not, in the interest of anthropology and phrenology and all the other 'ologies, pickle a few choice specimens of Bill Sikes to give our descendants an idea of what sort of individual he was.[56]

The more we progress the more we tend to progress. We advance not in arithmetical but in geometrical progression. We draw compound interest in the whole capital of knowledge and virtue which has been accumulated since the dawning of time. Some eighty thousand years intervened between Palaeolithic and Neolithic man, yet during that vast interval he only learned to grind his flintstones instead of clipping them. Yet in my own lifetime what improvement have I not witnessed! The railway train and the telegraph wire, chloroform and the telephone, with endless modifications and advances in every art and science. It is not too much to say that in ten years now we make as much progress as in a thousand years then, not on account of our finer intellects but because the light we have already gained helps us on to more. Primeval man stumbled along with peering eyes and slow uncertain footsteps – now we walk briskly down a broad and well-lit track which will lead us to some brilliant, though unknown, goal.

There is a sort of jackal-pessimist who goes about yelping
that civilisations have been built up before, and that this one of
ours may be no more permanent than that of Nineveh or of the
Aztecs. I deny that there was ever any old civilisation. Culture
depends on great sentiments, not on great buildings. An infinitude
of bricks and mortar, arches and frescoes, are no indication of
moral progress. Be they ever so wealthy and ever so industrious
in piling stones on stones, a nation which can rejoice in war, slay
its prisoners in cold blood, count it a holiday to see two poor
wretches slashing each other to pieces, believe devoutly in omens,
and allow every vice to flourish unchecked and unreproved,
cannot make any claim to civilisation. We have heard too much
of these vanished barbarians. The more we look back the less
likely we are to get on.

Again these scattered centres of pseudo-culture in olden days
only affected a small portion of the earth's area, and were hedged
in on every side by the fierce primitive peoples who eventually
overwhelmed them. We have no such danger to contend against.
Where is our enemy to come from, unless indeed John Chinaman
took it into his pigtailed head to run amuck against modern
progress? Far from doing so, he shows a strong tendency to snip
the pigtail off and to fall into line with the European nations.[57]
Look where we will, we cannot see any danger which can threaten
the growth of knowledge and of virtue. The two beautiful twin
sisters will increase and flourish to the end of time.

And what does it all lead up to? What is to be the end of it
all? Since first a man scratched hieroglyphics on an ostracon, or
scribbled with sepia upon a fragment of papyrus, the human race
has been puzzling itself over that question. We know a little more
– and only a little more – than did those original investigators.
We have an arc of three thousand years given us from which
to calculate the course to be described by our descendants, but
that arc is so tiny compared to the vast ages which Providence
uses in working out its designs, that our deductions from it must
be uncertain and imperfect. We may safely suppose, however,
that man will win fresh victories over mechanical and natural

difficulties. That he will navigate the air with the same ease and certainty with which he now does the water, and that his ships will travel under the waves as well as over them. That life will be rendered more refined and more pleasant by countless inventions, and that preventative medicine and sanitary science will work such wonders that accident and old age will be the only causes of death. That the common sense of nations will abolish war, and the education and improved social condition of communities will effect a marvellous diminution in crime. That the forms of religion will be abandoned but the essence maintained, so that one universal creed will embrace the whole earth, which shall preach reverence to the great Creator and the pursuit of virtue, not from any hope of reward or fear of punishment, but from a high and noble love of the right and hatred of the wrong.

These are some of the changes which may be looked for. And then? Why, by that time, perhaps the solar system will be ripe for picking. We are all piling up bricks under the direction of Providence, though we are too blind to know what sort of a temple we are helping to build. 'Ants see not the Pleiades' says the Persian poet Ferideddin Attar,[58] but the Pleiades are there all the same. At present we must do our duty as tools without hoping to share in the plans of the architect.

I wonder what has made me so very dogmatic and prophetic this morning! Perhaps it is the effect of the colchicum, or can it be the alkalis? It is really an excellent thing to take to writing when you are laid up. You see, if you chance to write well you can say that you did so *in spite of* your sickness, while if, as is more likely, you fail, then of course it was *on account of* your sickness. I am sure if ever I should chance to print these rambling notes the most stony-hearted critic would never venture to be severe on a man who was eight inches round the ankle. You may put all that is good down to me and all that is bad to the lithic acid.

If I were inclined (which, thank Heaven, I never was) to take a desponding view of human nature, I should have to change my lodgings before I could do it. It would be impossible for me to lie on this sofa with my face towards the window without recognising

that there are some of my fellow mortals who are treading so close
upon the heels of the angels that they won't have much to learn
when they take over their new duties. If there is a higher order of
being than a graceful, refined, self-sacrificing womanly woman,
it must be a very noble type indeed.

    She lives opposite, in the corresponding room on the other side
of the road – she and her old father. I can see all their movements
through the broad front window as plainly as though they were a
pair of Sir John Lubbock's ants,[59] enclosed in a glass prison for my
particular information and behoof. They have seen better days,
I should judge. He is quite the old-fashioned diplomatist, high-
collared, white-whiskered, eagle-faced – with many little courtly
airs and graces which sit well upon him in his own rooms. These
charms of manner are too often simply for export and not for home
consumption. The sitting room is poorly furnished, but when the
sun shines into it I can see little knick-knacks and ornaments, which
are relics no doubt of some larger and more luxurious household.
Very trim and neat she keeps them all, but with her utmost care
she can hardly make the dingy furniture and horsehair sofa look
anything but hideous. White-cuffed, black-dressed, quietly cheerful
and uncomplaining, I see her from morning to night planning
and striving with the one idea of smoothing the downward path
along which her old companion is journeying. Such women have
no separate existence of their own. They are Heaven's parasites,
and thrice lucky the man to whom they attach themselves!

    No, I don't think you could call her handsome. Trouble and
work and thought don't tend to produce regularity of feature. The
best souls, like the finest diamonds, are in the plainest settings.
If a woman reaches the age of thirty with perfectly symmetrical
features there must be a flaw either in her head or in her heart. My
vis-à-vis has a lithe graceful figure and a pale sweet long-suffering
face, which lights up into a loving smile when she addresses the
old man. Her hair is rich and brown with a coppery shimmer
when the sunshine strikes it. Did you ever observe the relation
between a woman's hair and her character – the quantity of her
hair, not the colour of it? I believe that there is a very direct ratio

between the two. A large-souled woman capable of great sacrifice and intense emotion may be long or short, pretty or plain, but in nine cases out of ten she has a wealth of hair. Thin and scraggy locks are a sign of a fickle and superficial soul. I have no doubt Dr Turner would pronounce it to be entirely a matter of circulation, but the fact is there all the same.

They are having a hard struggle to make both ends meet, those two, but the brunt of it falls upon her. He has usually an egg for breakfast, but a piece of bread and butter, or even I fear a piece of bread without the butter, is all her allowance. At their frugal dinner too I can see that she takes little herself that there may be more to support his failing strength. I declare that the sight makes me loathe my own well-cooked and savoury dishes – to think that I should have the means of pampering this old weather-beaten carcass of mine while that frail delicate creature is denying herself the necessaries of life! I must endeavour to find out something about them, but how? They have no visitors or friends of any sort. Perhaps Mrs Rundle may have gathered something from their landlady. There is a freemasonry among lodging-house keepers.[60] I shall call her up and enquire.

She knows a little but not much. The old gentleman's name is Oliver and he was the principal of a large private school in the provinces, but the local grammar school being heavily endowed and well-managed was able to undersell him until he could hold on no longer. His affairs were wound up and his creditors mercifully allowed him enough to sustain existence for the few short years which were left to him. 'And his daughter's a good young lady by all accounts,' continued Mrs Rundle. 'She ain't used to a life like that but she's that brave and sperrited that no one would never know as she'd been brought up anything better. She paints little pictures and sells 'em when she can at five shillings a piece – and well worth it too.'

'Does she though?' said I, seeing light at last. 'Here's a sovereign, Mrs Rundle. Just you run across and bespeak four of those pictures – for yourself, mind! Don't let my name be mentioned in the matter.'

'I'll go this very moment, sir,' said Mrs Rundle with sparkling eyes, and in five minutes I saw her cross the street and reappear in the little sitting room opposite, where I could see her bobbing about with excessive politeness and smiling all over her broad motherly face until the father and daughter laughed from sympathy. The message was soon delivered and as Mrs Rundle emerged from the hall door, I could see from my observatory that the girl bent over the old man and gave him a convulsive embrace and a passionate kiss. It was but the action of a moment and yet no words could have expressed more eloquently the vivifying effect of this one tiny streak of sunshine breaking through the clouds of her existence. It is extraordinary what an amount of pleasure may be had out of a sovereign if you know how to lay it out to advantage.

I wiled away an hour or so pleasantly this morning turning over the leaves of Samuel Carter Hall's reminiscences. If you have not read it, read it – if you have, read it again. It is a tonic in print, a glorious account of how ninety years may be strung upon the line of time like a row of pearls, each more lustrous and more valuable than its neighbour.[61] When I read it I would like to rub my fifty out and start again, as a man who has half finished his villa is tempted to pull it down and recommence when he sees the plans of a nobler and more commanding one. Who would speak with bated breath or wear the cursed black at the death of such a one? Let us mourn over a wasted life and weep over a worthless one, but with a man like this who has done his task bravely, his bed of death should be heaped with blossoms, friends with smiles and congratulations should press his wasted hands, and a blare of triumphant music should greet the young soul as it struggles out of the old husk which has clogged and obscured it so long. There is mirth at christenings and laughter at weddings, but no festival should be so merry as the death of a virtuous man. It is the one event in this world of ours which is entirely, undeniably and symmetrically auspicious.

Talking of Carter Hall's reminiscences, who can forget his anecdote of the absent-minded poetical clergyman who, when presenting a copy of the Bible to one of his parishioners, wrote

'With the author's compliments' upon the fly-leaf. He was so accustomed to giving away his little volumes of doggerel that the action was mechanical. There are a good many of his fellow clerics, however, who with all their wits about them assume an analogous attitude in the pulpit. Each would like to put his own petty hallmark upon the golden truth. 'This is so, and that is so – so far God's mercy extends and then it is superseded by his justice.' Steady, steady, my Christian friends! What private means of information have you upon that point? Preach a code of morality but for pity's sake leave dogma alone! Every one of you would like to write 'all rights reserved' across the covers of your own particular Bibles. Why pretend to be infallible exponents when you know that the meaning is obscure and that every man may fairly put his own interpretation upon it?

Oh for the inconsistencies of Anglican Protestant faith! Let it stand on its morality and on its results, but in the name of all that is true do not attempt to place it on the rigid foundation of biblical teaching! 'On the contrary, sir,' cries Dr Pontiphobus,[62] 'we take our stand entirely upon that ground.'

'And pray, my worthy Doctor, do you reckon transubstantiation to be an error?'

'Gross, sir, gross!'

'And yet if I mistake not Christ said, when he broke bread: "This is my body and this is my blood. This do in remembrance of me." You obey the latter half of the text but disbelieve the former.'

'Our blessed Saviour, sir,' says Dr Pontiphobus sternly, 'was speaking metaphorically upon that occasion. He never meant us to believe such a repulsive doctrine.'

'Oh indeed, Doctor, why do you practise baptism?'

'Why, sir, because our Saviour has most expressly said: "Unless ye be born again of water and the spirit, ye cannot enter into the kingdom of God."'

'He meant that, then?'

'We have no reason to think that he did not.'

'In fact, Doctor, whatever favours your creed he said literally, and whatever your creed rejects he said metaphorically – eh?'

'Sir,' says the Doctor, with odium theologicum in every feature, 'Augustine, Chrysostom and Tertullian have adduced one hundred and forty-nine reasons—' Let us fly, my friends, let us fly!

One other prod at the worthy Divine before we go. 'I presume, reverent sir, that the instructions which Christ gave to his disciples apply to all the clergymen who profess to be the present representatives of those disciples?'

'Undoubtedly they do.'

'And yet he said, Doctor, "Leave wife and child and follow me." How does that fit in with the existence of Mrs Pontiphobus and five little Pontiphobi? Oh Doctor, Doctor, claim what you will for the glorious Anglican Church, but not, for candour's sake, not entire consistency with the so-called Divine revelation.'

Don't imagine that I am pleading for celibacy of the clergy. I am pointing out an inconsistency, not defending a doctrine. In theory there is no doubt that the man who has no earthly encumbrances, and whose thoughts are not tied down to earth by the necessity of continually providing for the maintenance of a household and the comfort of a family, is likely to be the most efficient servant of a Church. But in practice it is a dangerous doctrine. Celibacy may produce a saint and it may produce a devil. It may raise a man among the angels or it may sink him among the beasts. Have we a right to play head-or-tails with a man's soul in that fashion?

It was a cursed day when religion as taught by Christ was changed into religion as understood by Christians. Well has Froude said that the gospel comes from God but theology was invented by the devil. Well done, John Anthony, you have spoken a true and a brave word there.[63] The simple self-denying life, the broad reforming spirit, the humble tender heart are all of Heaven, but the narrow tenets of our modern churches, the creeds and articles, the dogmas, the anathemas and the excommunications – they are weapons from the armoury of Gehenna. When religion is weeded of all forms of evangelistic gossip, and is founded upon elemental truth, there will be some hope of ending the petty bickerings of creeds, and of including the whole human family in one comprehensive faith.

These elemental truths are easily arrived at without the aid of book or preceptor. If a man could be born alone into the world, and could in spite of his isolation acquire a moderate degree of reasoning power, he would be able to evolve from his own resources a religion which, if less highly elaborated than our present ones, would at least be less open to criticism. Let us imagine this solitary philosopher and let us see how he arrives at his conclusions. Experience would soon convince him that there was never an effect without a cause – that wherever in the woods there was a nest, there must have been a nest-maker. Given a world, then, there could be no question that a world-maker existed, and a glance at the starry firmament would convince him that this maker must be a being of enormous and infinite power. Already, you see, our lonely man has attained to the idea of an omnipotent Creator. But he would soon get further than that. He could not wander through the woods in springtime and watch how bird, beast and plant have all been cared for, and had their wants foreseen and provided for, without realising that this maker was infinitely kind as well as infinitely powerful, and that no detail of his handiwork was so small as to escape him. Having attained this conception of the goodness of his Maker, shown in his own case by the rich grain and blooming fruits which lay ready for the plucking, it is but natural that he should conceive a respectful affection for the unseen cause, and that he should offer up thanks to him. So here we have our man praying to an all-merciful and omnipotent invisible Creator – and that without any teaching except the lessons contained in the broad, clearly inscribed pages of Nature. But now we come to a dangerous point in our lonely reasoner's spiritual education. His idea of an all-kind father receives a severe shock when he observes that there are occasional phases of Nature which are by no means kind, but on the contrary which appear to him to be entirely malignant and vicious. The lightning splits and blasts the young oak, the hurricane beats down the rising grain, the icy winds blight the flowers and cut him to the very bone. How is this hard inexorable mood to be explained? Can it be made to tally with his original conception of infinite tenderness? There are only two lines of thought open to him. He may conceive the existence of a second spirit, evil in its nature, which occasionally asserts itself in the affairs of the world, or he may imagine that these things, although they appear objectionable to us, really serve some good end, and that they fulfill some necessary function in the grand scheme of Creation although our mortal eyes are too dim to understand what it is.

Having attained this point by the examination of all that was around him he would complete the evolution of his religion by turning his thoughts to his own internal consciousness with its subtle whisperings and promptings. Many thoughts and impulses he would find, some swaying him this way and some swaying him that, but over them all would sit Reason, the calm inflexible Judge, telling him that all were not alike but that there was good and bad in his own nature, even as he had seen it in the larger nature around him. 'It is good to be kind to the poor helpless animals,' says Reason, 'for He who made you made them, and He gave you no permission to ill-use them. If He has been thoughtful of them, why should you be otherwise? It is good for the same reason to treat your fellow men with consideration should you ever chance to fall in with such. Gluttony is bad and so is drunkenness, for are you not ill after an excess, and illness enfeebles and degrades that body which has been made by the greatest of Architects.' Thus would the solitary man build up a moral code as well as a religious belief, and without attaining the conception of a heaven or a hell he would humbly acknowledge himself to be a tool in the Master's hand, and would do such duties as came in his way without fear and without question, obeying as far as he could fathom it the will of his Maker, not from any base hope of reward but from an inward sense of duty, and sustained the while by a deep-seated conviction that there was some destiny in store for him, and that the good Father would not treat his poor, tired workman in a scurvy fashion. This is elemental religion by which a man may build up for himself such a faith as is set down in the grand comprehensive verse of Micah. 'And what doth the Lord require of thee but to do justly and to love mercy and to walk humbly with thy God.' It is a bald creed with no lurid hells or shining heavens, no original sins, or water-cleansings or wine-drinkings, or even any cogent necessity for the piling up of stones, or the ringing of bells; but it has the advantage that every link of it may be readily tested and rings true – so true that all future discoveries and sciences and philosophies can never materially alter it. There will be some grand movement soon in the direction of a purer and simpler creed. The old religions are mostly dead, and some of them have begun to putrefy.

Kant remarked that two things always filled him with awe and admiration: the moral sense within him and the stars above him. 'Nature proves,' says Jean Paul Richter,[64] 'that there is a creator, and history that there is a Providence.' Those two observations contain the true core of all religions, and innumerable cut-and-dried dogmas or tawdry formalities will not advance us a hairbreadth. Oh that a man should take his religion as he does his name or the colour of his hair from his parents! How can advance be made while such a custom prevails? I do not envy the man who can treat a problem of such gravity in so haphazard a style, and can save himself thought by taking refuge behind ten generations of ancestors. Who would be ready to appeal to his grandfather upon questions of astronomy, of geography, of medicine? In this one grandest of all questions, however, nineteenth-century man is content to be stagnant, stuck up to the neck in the mud of the centuries, without advance or hope of advance. It is time that some few made a struggle to get out of the quagmire and to gain a more solid footing – but, alas, what a dead-weight of stolid, thoughtless humanity they will have to pull after them. I fear that they will be mostly content with having emancipated their own minds, and will throw the task down, exclaiming with Schiller, *Gegen die dummheit kämpfen die Götter selbst vergebens.*[65]

'Shake a man's faith!' That is one of those ridiculous phrases which continues to pass current in the world, however often it is proved to be base metal and nailed to the counter of truth. Shake a man's faith! Why, if it is shakable, the sooner he examines into it and either abandons it or else fortifies it, so as to render it less insecure, the better for him and the better for all. Of what practical value is a faith which is so delicate that it must be screened off from every gust of controversy? What does a citizen reply to his neighbour who comes to warn him that the bank in which he has placed his capital is by no means secure? Does he place his fingers in his ears and scream hysterically, 'My father dealt with that bank before me. Oh, do not shake my faith in the bank!'? On the contrary, he thanks his neighbour, if he is a man of sense, and putting aside all preconceived ideas of the bank, he sets himself to examine how it now is, and whether his capital is in safety. The fact is that in spite of all loud-tongued assertions to the contrary, the human race does not take as keen or personal an interest in the choice of a religion as in the choice of an investment. When they are too lazy to question, they take credit for having an unquestioning faith. They find, like the American humourist, that they are saddest when they think.[66]

And when a man does from time to time stand up and protest against the great mangled mutilated creed, which is professed by four hundred denominations which are ever at one another's throats as not being the *ne plus ultra* of religion, what a howling and a cat-calling there is from the poor mud-stuck wretches! How cheap it is to earn a reputation for piety by crying down the earnest enquirer, even as the Pharisees strutted about, reeking with virtue, when they had done to death the great radical reformer. Do you remember the story of the two European travellers who found their way to a village in South America where the inhabitants were all afflicted with goitre and had never seen a healthy man? The stunted, deformed wretches crowded round their visitors, pointing sardonically at them with derisive fingers and screaming, 'They have no goitre! They have no goitre!' So accustomed were they to the sight of their own hideous malformation that a healthy man appeared to them to be repulsive and grotesque. So a man who has had his mind trammelled and confined from his infancy, until it is as shrunken in its religious aspect as a Chinese lady's foot, mocks and menaces when he sees a free healthy soul tasting all that is put before it, and exercising all the gifts with which the

Great Creator has endowed it. Bring to the consideration of such questions a mind as plastic as wet plaster of Paris, but, having once formed your convictions, let it set as hard.

Conceive the great founder of the Christian religion returning in the flesh to this England of ours and walking down the Surrey side of the Thames, much interested in the noble river and in the bustling scenes around him. Presently he comes to a noble wide-spread building, tower-flanked and palatial, from the arched door of which there drives a handsome carriage containing an elderly, well-fed gentleman who is setting off for the House of Lords. 'Pray, who is the owner of this great house?' Christ asks of a bystander. 'The Archbishop of Canterbury.' 'And who is he?' continues the enquirer. 'Why, he is the representative in England of Christ of Nazareth who was crucified nearly two thousand years ago.' Christ would look up at the gorgeous palace with its countless windows, and would look back at the dim-lit, low-roofed carpenter's shop in which he spent the first thirty years of his life, and of the roving precarious existence which terminated on Calvary. Then he would glance after the rolling carriage and would recall the days when he rode his shaggy-haired old donkey into Jerusalem, or wore his sandals out by tramping over the countryside. A strange sort of representative this, truly!

But this would be only the beginning of his experience of the strange developments of Christianity. What is this howling, drum-beating band which comes surging down the Embankment? Here are red-vested men and tambourine-playing women waving, shouting, shrieking, gesticulating, with flushed faces and the wild light of fanaticism in their eyes. Christ steps aside, under the impression that he has come across some party of drunken revellers, or some private asylum perhaps out for its daily airing. As the noisy crowd goes by, however, he touches one of them upon the shoulder and asks who he and his companions may be. 'We are the soldiers and followers of Christ of Nazareth,' cries the fellow. 'Do you come with us and be saved?' At the words, the whole howling gang turn upon the mild-faced stranger and would have borne him away forcibly with them had he not escaped them by darting into a small brick building, the door of which happened to be ajar.[67]

A red-bearded man is preaching inside to a select meeting of the Chosen primitive Trinitarians.[68] The august visitor stands at the bottom of the bare, whitewashed Chapel and listens. 'We are the chosen of Christ,' says the hard-faced minister. 'Oh, my brethren, how can we thank him enough? *We* are not condemned to outer darkness as are the unbelievers and the heathen. *We* are not participators in the idolatry of the Mass, as are the hypocritical and bloody-minded Papists. *We* are not as those of the English Church who are rich in lawn and linen and all good things, but shall assuredly be cast, bound hand and foot, into the pit. *We* are not outcasts as are Wesleyans, Baptists and all others beyond our own fold. It is true that we are very few in number, but to us alone has God reserved the kingdom of heaven – ' 'And is this the outcome of my sublime doctrine of Universal charity!' cries Christ, and hurries away, sick at heart.

Who should come in to see me this afternoon but the old officer who lives above me – a hatchet-faced, grizzly featured old gentleman with a skin tanned by many climates, and a slight limp from a Jezail bullet in the knee.[69] For all his experiences and hardships he is as merry and as elastic in his spirits as a boy. I am not generally disposed to take to military men, recognising in them a certain pride of caste which is not warranted by their services to humanity, but his kindly, grey eyes and his frank apologies for what he called his intrusion won my heart at once.

'A man gets down on his luck when he's seedy,' said he. 'His mind gets a little morbid unless someone drops in and stirs him up. You don't mind my lunkah, do you? I've been a confirmed smoker all my life, and I've never shirked my liquor. Yet I'm pretty well preserved for sixty-one – preserved in spirits, some people would say, eh?' He laughed a creaking wheezy laugh at his own little joke, and lay back in my easy chair with his long thin legs stretched out and a thick cloud of blue smoke ascending from him.

'I dare say that you have seen a good deal of sickness during your career, Major,' I observed.

'Seen a good deal and had a good deal,' said he. 'I had the devil of a dose of dysentery in the Afghan passes. They invalided me for that. I have had yellow Jack at Sierra Leone, malarious fever at Port Royal, and cholera at Shanghai. I can tell you that the British flag flies over a finer assorted collection of diseases than any nation can boast of. We are always talking of the resources and products of the Empire, but you don't hear much of that side of the question. Britain produces the men and the Empire consumes them. Many a tall fellow has left his bones in Indian and African graves who ought in the course of nature to be now walking over the moors of Yorkshire or the Downs of Sussex. The great machine won't run unless it's greased with British lives.'

'It is worth a sacrifice to preserve it,' said I, 'for the sun never shone on so grand a heritage as that which we are handing down to our descendants.'

'No,' said the Major thoughtfully. 'No monarch on this earth ever had so many subjects as has Queen Victoria. They are a mixed lot, however, and will take a powerful deal of welding together. As long as the heart keeps right I have no fear for the limbs, but if once this tight little island of ours went wrong there would soon be gangrene in the extremities, and amputation of one or two of them might be needed to strengthen the rest. I hope I may not live to see the day. I have spent my life in helping to build it up, and I don't want to see it undone before I die.'

Now this should be a lesson to me never again to judge a man rashly! From the little I had seen and heard of my fellow lodger I had conceived a poor opinion of him, and had thought more than once how objectless an existence his had been. Yet I find him upon closer acquaintance to be kind-hearted, intelligent and full of a noble purpose. If he has at times cheered his monotonous and solitary life by an extra glass of grog, which has made his old tongue wag faster and his heart beat stronger, who am I that I should blame him?

'I should like to see a little more transfusion in the Empire,' he remarked after a pause. 'More black faces in the streets of London and more white ones in the country parts of India. We should find billets in England for a thousand bright Hindoo youths every year, and send out as many of our own young fellows to work at the tea and indigo. It would help us towards consolidating the union between the countries. A few Indian regiments in English garrison towns would have the same effect. As to our parliament, it should be a piebald assembly with every hue from jet to brown, red and yellow, with occasionally a bronze-coloured premier at the head of them. What's the odds how much pigment a man has in his skin, if he has a level head and a loyal heart. Gad, sir, I've seen our British regiments glad enough of their help on the day of battle – why shouldn't we be equally ready to have their assistance at our councils? The Aryan conquerors of England need not be ashamed to take into partnership the Aryan conquerors of India, even though their hide has been a little burned by their long stay in the tropics. Excuse my flying off at a tangent, won't you? A lonely man gets so much thought bottled up in him that when he does open his mouth it just foams out of him. How is your ankle now?'

'It darts a little from time to time,' I answered.

'And so does my knee, so we can condole with each other. It's rheumatic weather. I can see that Afreedee now, with his seven-foot gun laid across a rock and his black eyes twinkling behind the sights.[70] I saw that the rascal was aiming at me, and I made for him as hard as I could, but he rolled me over like a shot rabbit when I was about twenty paces off. A Sergeant of ours had his bayonet through his lungs before he had time to make off. Ugh, it's a bad business is war – a very bad business.'

'So bad,' said I, 'that unless in case of actual attack I cannot conceive how any war can be justified.'

'Well, well,' said the old soldier rising and throwing the stump of his cigar into the grate, 'that is for the authorities to decide. If they are wrong – why, the responsibility rests with them. It isn't for the troops to begin moralising about their orders. I've often thought that if statesmen had seen a little real fighting they would not declare war with such a light heart. As for us, if we are ordered to Cabul, why to Cabul we must go, if the whole seven deadly sins stood in the way. Besides, wars and pestilences are the prunings of Providence. Perhaps the human tree grows better when its branches are freely lopped. That's camp-fire philosophy.[71] Goodbye. I'll look in from time to time if I don't bore you, and see how you get on.'

CHAPTER 3

THE DEMON has let go of my ankle this morning but has clutched me by the wrist with his red-hot paw and has left the part hot and pringling. A thick, yellow vapour rolls sluggishly down the street, hanging in heavy folds about the house-tops, as though a great counterpane had been spread over the sleeping city. Solid mud, liquid mud, volatilized mud – all is dreary and miserable.[72] Clearly it is not a day when any sensible disease could be induced to take its departure out of a warm, comfortable human economy. I must wait with such patience as I may, consoling myself with the fact that I can hobble about the room now without any particular pain.

There is an empty house at the other side of the street which has a depressing effect upon me.[73] There is a deep-lying sense of the fitness of things in every man's nature, which causes a vague feeling of annoyance and irritation when his eye rests upon that which is profitless and useless. An idle man, a closed factory, a laid-up vessel and an untenanted house have all something repugnant in them. This particular house stares across at me with two great glassy vacuous eyes, in one of which a cataract has developed in the shape of a 'to let' card. If I were a richer man I would pay for a caretaker in order to put some soul into the empty body.

As the fog lifts, I can make out that my little friend opposite is hard at work upon the paintings. Poor lass, she goes to work with as much care and importance upon her face as though she had been entrusted with a thousand-pound commission. She has her little easel and her canvas, her colours and her brushes – the latter all new from the colour-shop in honour of the great order which she has received. They are all set out with much precision and nicety. Now she comes over to the window, and sits with her much-troubled meditative head supported on her hands. What is her subject to be? Here is a great and weighty question for one small woman to decide. She wonders, no doubt, what Mrs Rundle's particular taste in art may be. Good Mrs R as a matter of fact would admire the coloured supplement to the *Graphic* in a new frame very much more than she would the 'Assumption' of Murillo in an old one – but then my little friend does not know that. She must think my landlady an ardent connoisseur and art-critic, otherwise why should she lay out so large a sum upon original paintings when she might get a grand, flaring oleograph,[74] like a spectrum analysis, for half the money, containing all the colours in nature laid on with a brilliancy which Nature has not yet been able to arrive at. Hullo, the head comes up, and she looks hard across at our house, running her eye over the whole front. Ha, my dear, I can read your thoughts! You are wondering whether a picture of this dingy smoke-dried old edifice would be acceptable to its owner. Apparently the inspection is not satisfactory, for down goes the anxious head again. Shall it be a 'girl at the well,' or a 'woodland scene' or the 'village green'? The old gentleman is looking anxiously at her over the top of his newspaper, fearing perhaps with the petty selfishness of age that she may give the thing up in despair, and that the precious sovereign will have to be returned. At last, however, she has an idea and gets fairly to work, to her companion's evident relief. It is a landscape, I should judge, from the long sweeping strokes.

By the way, I trust she won't draw a fishing boat or anything appertaining to one. No doubt they are very picturesque objects but when one has seen about fifty thousand of them, drawn in fifty thousand styles by fifty thousand different artists, one's thirst for them becomes satiated. If I should never see another I should not pine for want of them. 'Arrival of a smack in a storm.' That was the title of one of the pictures in a small colonial collection, but on looking up expecting to see the inevitable brown lug-sail and bearded mariner I was agreeably surprised to find that the sketch represented a domestic disagreement which had ended by the strong-minded wife administering what is known to the fancy[75] as a 'nose-ender' to her unfortunate spouse.[76] The idea was original and the artistic handling superb. The middle distance was effectively portrayed and the chiaro-obscuro all that could be desired. The management of the light and shade, especially of the light of resentment in her eye, and of the shade which some previous attack had left upon her husband's optic, was remarkably effective. The arrangement of the lady's drapery, and the power of perspective and foreshortening by which the artist expressed the flattening of the most prominent feature of the gentleman's countenance, reminded us of Fra Angelico at his best. Some little blame must however be mixed with our own praise. The table in the centre of the room has a decidedly wooden look, the poker is somewhat stiff and there is a want of spirit about the empty gin bottle upon the mantelpiece. There now – after that I think when this gout leaves me I shall apply for the billet of art-critic for any of our learned weeklies.

The Colonies! Ah me, what a flood of memories and thoughts and regrets the word brings with it! What recollections of sad days and of happy ones, of good men and of bad, of flush times and of misery. There is no dead-level of existence over there. Fortune shuffles up the cards pretty often and at every deal the game fluctuates and changes. The best men and the worst that I have ever known live under the Southern Cross. All Old England's best flowers and all her worst weeds have been carried across the seas.

I was a very young fellow at the time of the gold-rush in Australia[77] and the harum-scarum happy-go-lucky life suited my Bohemian disposition to a nicety.[78] One needs the elasticity of youth to stand an existence of that kind. When a man's cartilage has all turned to bone he does not adapt himself to circumstances with the same readiness. Sheep-tending and cattle-driving, digging at Ballarat and bursting the proceeds at Melbourne on bad spirits at a guinea a bottle are all occupations which are a little trying to the constitution. Worst of all was it when, having paraded up and down Collins Street for a week or two, getting rid of our money with both hands, we found ourselves some fine morning with empty pockets and with no means of returning to the mines or of travelling up country. We would lie by then in the slums, living as best we could and waiting for some lucky chance, or the advent of some trustful 'new chum' with lending proclivities, to provide us with the means of getting back to our work.

The incidents of one of these intervals of enforced idleness – most spirit-subduing of all conditions – are still fresh in my recollection. There were four of us, all penniless, all waiting for something to turn up, and all sleeping at night in empty hogsheads or any other shelter we could find. One of our number was an Englishman of good birth who retained through all his colonial experiences a drawl, an eyeglass, a pair of long Dundreary whiskers, and even some appearance of fashion in the cut of his old coat and threadbare trousers. One night, hungry and cheerless, we met together and found that among the four of us we had just money enough to provide some sort of coarse meal. The small sum was handed over with many exhortations and admonitions to our English swell, who advanced boldly into one of the principal butcher's shops while we stood palpitating outside. With jaunty step, flourishing cane, and eyeglass duly adjusted, our ambassador swaggered round the shop pricing the primest joints in a lordly way while the tradesman waited respectfully for his commands. 'You've nothing over two shillings a pound, hey?' asked the customer sternly. 'That is our price for prime joints, sir.' 'And what do you charge for – aw – lights, hey?' 'Four pence a pound, sir,' said the tradesman in surprise. 'Then weigh me out three pounds of lights,' said our swell, laying a shilling upon the counter. He was leaving with his purchase when the butcher, unable to restrain his astonishment any longer, exclaimed, 'Surely, sir, you are not going to eat that!' 'I have a dawg,' explained our messenger as he hurried out with his parcel to where his three hungry and impatient companions were eagerly awaiting him. 'I have a dawg' became a sort of cant phrase in the camp after that, whenever anyone wished to put the blame of his actions upon another.[79]

I remember that the sailors of a merchant vessel which was

unloading sacks of potatoes on Melbourne quay were surprised
to see our aristocratic-looking friend leaning against their pile
of bags and watching them through his eyeglass as they worked.
They may have thought it an act of condescension on the part of
this gaudy mortal that he should take an interest in their labours.
When they discovered afterwards that he had slit one of the bags
with his penknife and that he had departed with his coat tails and
his high hat crammed full of their vegetables, they were probably
less gratified at his notice. I don't know that these little vignettes
of the past are of much interest to anyone, but they may serve
to add a dash of life to the day book of an invalid. In those wild
old days we were not very strait-laced, but we managed to get a
good deal of amusement out of life. You remember the American
Humourist's wise and witty aphorism: 'Virtuous people are happy
– but they are never *very* happy.' That may, however, be balanced
by the fact that the virtuous man, conscious of his own integrity,
can never be wholly and completely miserable.

Talking of humour, how very difficult it is to define in what
that very subtle quality consists or whence it comes. I have been
reading of late Emerson's 'Essay upon the Comic,' and very sad
and depressing reading it is.[80] To explain a joke is proverbially
dangerous but to analyse one and to show by hard rules why we
should laugh and when we should laugh is a prelude to melancholy
madness. Yet when a man, on account of certain words falling
upon his tympanum, is straightway taken with violent spasms
of his diaphragm and convulsions of every muscle of his body,
accompanied by hideous facial grimaces and considerable uproar, it
is only natural that he and his friends should desire to know what
the cause of the phenomenon might be. Supposing that only one
mortal was endowed with the sense of humour and that all the rest
of the human race was uniformly grave, what consultations would
be held, and clinical lectures delivered, whenever the humorous
one indulged in an outburst of merriment. In that case laughter
would be placed among the nervous diseases somewhere between
hysteria and epilepsy, and large doses of asafoetida and bromide
of potassium would soon take the fun out of the patient.

How strange to trace the course of a joke in the human economy. Entering through the eye or ear, it travels along the optic or auditory nerve to the brain where it is referred to some special humourous centre – which, by the way, is wanting in five men and nine women out of every ten. Thence it travels at the ascertained rate of 147 feet per second (*vide* Rutherford on nerve force[81]) along the great jocular or phrenic nerve, until it reaches the diaphragm or breathing muscle which separates the chest from the abdomen. This great muscle, responding to the nervous stimulus, begins to contract violently – and that's where the laugh comes in.

When you hear of a politician exclaiming 'that thousands of pounds are being squandered upon education, while many a poor man in the country has not money enough to buy whisky,' or when you read that the sentence 'Mr Gladstone has burned his boats and his bridges' has been reported in the daily papers as 'Mr Gladstone has burned his coats and his breetches,' you feel inclined to laugh. It is the unexpected and novel character of each assertion which produces this effect, just as an unexpected finger poked between your ribs makes you squirm and writhe. Again, when Mr Clemens[82] tells us 'never to put off till tomorrow what we can possibly postpone until the day after tomorrow,' it is clearly the daring unconventionality of the remark which sets us tittering. Emerson recognises this element of surprise in the Comic. Carlyle, who had a vein of grim but very genuine humour in his composition, defines the quality as being 'a sympathy with the underside' – a description which is subtle to the verge of incomprehensibility. Old Thomas was never very strong on definitions. His explanation of Genius, as being 'an infinite capacity for taking pains,' has been often quoted, but is, I take it, the most symmetrically and completely false definition which has ever been advanced, though as a statement of what genius is *not* it is crisp and concise.[83] I have only known one or two men in my life who might come under the category, and the predominant features of their characters were that they had the power of arriving at results intuitively and instinctively, which would cost other men much trouble and labour.[84] Genius is a strong inborn hereditary mental aptitude in any particular direction.

What is humour? – what is genius? I'll give you a third, and a tougher and more vital conundrum. What is instinct? When we have made that point clear we shall have gained a master-key which will open up a good many of the secrets of nature.

Why is it that the young chicken begins to peck, the pointer to point or the baby to suck without requiring any tuition? Though use has blunted our appreciation of instinct, this is one of the most mysterious of problems. No one has communicated to this dog, chicken or baby what they are to do, and yet they set to work of their own accord exactly as their parents did before them. The young creature, considered individually and alone, can know nothing of the uses of the organs with which Nature has endowed it. Any knowledge it has can only come from its being one of a series and from its being so closely connected with its ancestors that their experience is practically its experience also.

What is instinct then? You know how Edwin Arnold answers the question in one of the most brilliant of his essays.[85] 'Instinct is memory,' says he – as pregnant a combination of three words as ever was put together. Instinct is memory. This puppy who points is no new dog but one who has lived through all the centuries – a graft from the life of her mother, who was a graft from the life of her mother and so through countless ages. When we view the lower forms of animal life the truth of the principle becomes apparent. The amoeba is a little morsel of colourless jelly which propagates its species by dividing down the centre and so splitting into two young amoeba, each of which having grown to the size of their parent repeats the process of generation. Now in the case of this simple organism it is quite plain that the creature is eternal, and that the amoeba of today is not only a descendant of the amoeba of prehistoric time, but is actually the same creature. The amoeba cannot die. So in the case of higher and more complex forms of life, although the method of generation is less primitive, it may be none the less true that the individual is eternal. That our memory can recall little of a former existence is hardly surprising when we consider how dim and imperfect is our recollection of the first few years of the very life which we are leading now.

What a weight Arnold's theory imparts to the most trivial things – if anything can be said to be trivial in this universe! The chicken which scrapes in our backyard is no creature of yesterday but is the primitive fowl, hatched in the dawn of the ages and destined to live until the close of time – though the little empty head is too busy with worm-seeking and grain-picking to be conscious of its ever-recurring existences. Even in that picking and seeking, however, it shows us plainly that it has acquired knowledge which can only be referred to some foregoing experience.

There is a remark of Crabbe Robinson in his highly interesting journal which has a bearing on this subject. 'We can hardly allow a future eternity,' says he, 'without supposing that we have eternally existed. A thing could not be created in time for eternity.'[86] That statement has a ring of truth about it and, taken with Arnold's theory, supplies food for much high thought. It is time to get onto another siding, though, or we may find ourselves in dark places.

I wish Science would try and make up her mind as to what is and what is not true. I object to the scientific bully with his mouth full of figures and statistics, who reeks with contempt if he finds that you believe in the theory of yesterday and yet is ready to commit assault and battery upon you if you hint that his explanation of today may not be absolutely final. Couldn't our scientific friends draw up two tables, one of what they know for certain and the other of what is open to question? I am afraid the printer wouldn't have a very big job in striking off the first, though he might exhaust his stock of paper over the other. I don't care about taking a tenant into my brain, and then just when he is snugly settled down, finding him to be worthless and having to evict him.[87]

Now take the sun for example.[88] Ever since I first took to milk I have had it driven into me that the sun was an enormous mass of burning matter, which warmed us just as any other great fire would do. When I grew up I read voluminous scientific treatises which reasserted and confirmed the teachings of the nursery. Have I not committed to memory the weight of the sun, and the amount of fuel which that weight represents, and how long it will last, and what will happen when it snuffs out – together with gorgeous descriptions of incandescent hydrogen and molten helium and other such madness? What details have I not collected together, and docketed and stored away in the pigeon-holes of my memory to the exclusion of other matter? And what is the end of it all? Why, the other day, happening to babble some of this information to a friend well posted in modern science, he looked at me with as much interest as if I were a *Calopterus gracilis* or some other curious fossil. 'There are still people alive then,' said he, 'who believe that the sun is on fire.' 'I always thought so,' said I, feeling particularly small. 'My dear fellow,' he observed compassionately, 'it is a vulgar error which has exploded some time ago. If it were on fire, where are the stokers who trim it so carefully that it never blazes too much or too little – more on this side or on that? Where are the ashes produced by such a combustion? Where is the oxygen to feed the flame? Where is the—' 'But where does the heat come from?' I cried. 'Why, it is generally supposed by advanced scientists to arise from an electrical influence which the sun exercises upon our atmosphere. A galvanic battery will heat a wire at a distance but does not become hot itself. It's the same with the sun. The heat of a fire won't pass through glass and the heat of the sun will. That shows that they are entirely different. Don't let anyone know that you thought the sun was on fire or they'll wonder where you have been shut up all this time.' 'It's a mean fraud,' said I indignantly. 'Here have I been reckoning up how many billion tons of fuel there are left, and bustling round to do what I could to keep it alight, and waking up at night in a fright for fear it should want looking after, and now it turns out that, as like as not, it is a glittering iceberg.' It shook my confidence in the solar system. I have never felt the same towards the sun since, and I never will again.

Seriously though, if Science were a little more modest and less dogmatic she would not expose her humble followers to such shocks as the above. We cannot all have Lord Rosse's telescopes in our garrets and verify every observation for ourselves.[89] If savants tell us that a point is settled, we forthwith absorb it into systems, and we feel ill-used when, in the course of a few years, we have to disgorge it again. We stand on a very narrow basis of ascertained fact, with vast untouched sciences looming upon us through the darkness. Look at electricity with its vast possibilities; magnetism an inexplicable phenomenon which dominates all nature and is as universal as gravity; mesmerism with its suggestions of a sixth sense which may be developing in the human race. In each of these subjects there is a field for tyro Newtons. What is light and what is heat? What is the subtle elastic medium which pervades all space and which conducts light without being itself illuminated? Are there many unknown elements, or are those which we acknowledge capable of being resolved into a very few, which form the original clay out of which Nature manufactured her bricks? When the human race has solved all these problems, they will still be only nibbling at the borders of knowledge.

Our accurate information about the intimate organisation of our own human bodies is pitifully small when one thinks of the immense amount of labour which has been expended over it. Physiology is a science which is richer in polysyllables than in facts. Our learned professors can tell us occasionally what an organ is made for, and even make some guess at how it acts, but what satisfaction can he give us as to the motive power? The most ordinary phenomena of life are sealed books to us, however much we may mask our ignorance by sonorous words and solemn countenances.

Did it ever strike you how calmly we acquiesce in the phenom-enon of sleep and how completely ignorant we are of what the immediate cause of it may be? How strange that our scientists should spend their days in investigating all manner of morbid rarities, the beri-beri of India or the Lata of Sumatra, and should never attempt an explanation as to why the human race spends one third of its time in a profound trance! There is something amusing in our disregard for all that is familiar to us. The physician sits down at his study table with a rash upon his face and his stomach full of wind, and he writes a forty-page pamphlet on Addison's disease of Ichthyosis, as well as the pains in his epigastrium will allow him. You would imagine that he would be inclined to look into this little complaint of his own which is rendering the lives of so many of his fellow mortals unhappy, but no, he is bound to go off in pursuit of some gaudy disease which appears about once a century, and is then so like some other disease that no one can tell them apart. Look over any weekly medical paper and you will find that nine paragraphs out of ten are devoted to complaints which no man of simple tastes would ever dream of contracting.

This question of sleep, however, always seems to me to be a glaring example of how very shallow our enquiries are. Why is it that I spend so much of my time in a state of insensibility? 'It is because Nature must recruit herself – it is to act as a restorative to the system – it is because the brain is less vascular than during waking hours – it is because action and rest are inseparable terms.' Quite so. In fact I go to sleep because I go. I might have struggled to that conclusion without any learned friend at my elbow.

Now I will tell you why you go to sleep. In moving or thinking or even in merely existing there is always a chemical change going on in our system, and the waste products are removed from the muscles or nerves by the blood. Now, among the many complex chemicals which exist among these waste products and which find their way into the circulation, there is one which is a narcotic poison. This is slowly evolved during the process of tissue change, but in from twelve to sixteen hours it accumulates to such an extent in the system that it produces its characteristic effects. Some agents, as opium, chloral and alcohol, favour the formation of this important substance while others such as green tea or black coffee neutralise its action. In sleep, as the system is in complete rest, very little of the narcotic-containing tissue-waste is formed and the constitution has an opportunity of shaking off all that has accumulated – through the skin and kidneys – hence the individual wakes refreshed. Have you never noticed the characteristic smell of a sleeping person? That comes from the fact that every pore of his skin is exhaling this subtle compound. There is a brand-new original theory for you! What's that? Why should a narcotic send people to sleep? Why, of course – I'll let you know some other time when I have a week or two to spare.

No signs of Dr Julep today which looks as if he does not take a very serious view of my case.[90] I know that I am working the thing off, but still I should be more satisfied if I had it through what the newspapers call 'the ordinary official channels.' This little day-book of mine is a sufferer through his absence for, as you have seen, he is a chatty genial mortal and has generally something to say which is worth making a note of. With the exception of the sudden intrusion of the slavey's head with an abrupt 'Please, sir, Missus wants to know whether you'll take parsnips or turnips?', I have been abandoned entirely to myself. I console myself however by making spiritual excursions over the way and sliding down a sunbeam into that little chamber where the great art contract is being carried out. She has finished one, I perceive, and has made a good deal of progress with another. I am puzzled as to what I shall do with them when they come over. It would be hardly fair to hang them beside any William Blake, Doré and De Neuville.

In the intervals between jotting down these rambling notes I have picked up a couple of novels from the circulating library, but they are not very absorbing reading. They are both of the good old crusted order, where the conventional heroine, having lost her heart to the conventional hero, is prevented by a number of conventional events from recovering that organ until the conclusion of the third volume. There is an atmosphere of curl-papers and kid gloves about them, but where is the warm human life, with its frail impulses and its curious way of saying and doing exactly what you least expect? Now, I'll wager that if I were to take the two gentlemen who wrote these books into any drawing room and there bring them into contact with people who talked exactly as they represent their characters as talking, they would set them down as the most intolerable prigs they ever met. Let us take an example haphazard from these two text books. 'Ah, Miss Mortimer,' exclaimed George Stephen, raising his Tam o'Shanter cap. 'Your eyes are the sun and your smile the warmth which revives everyone around you.' Even in print that has rather a solid sound, but if you try to say it to a young lady you will find that no ordinary girl could bear up against it. 'My dear friend,' said the Colonel as he filled his glass, 'let us throw aside all gloomy anticipations and form a fixed resolution to stand by each other whatever the future may bring forth—' A very sonorous Colonel, but not a very natural one.

It is very seldom in real conversation that you hear a long sentence, or a sentence containing a parenthesis. The average man has no great command of language and would no more dream of interlarding his talk with neat similes and happy allusions than he would of dancing into a room instead of walking into it. In most dialogues each sentence consists of a very few words, and when the speaker wishes to amplify, he does it by fresh sentences and not by bloating a single one out with conjunctions until it is like one of these Chinese boxes, which contains a dozen more inside it, each within the other. Now here's an interview between an old country squire and his promising son, as described by a novelist and as reported by a shorthand reporter. You will observe that the real conversation is a good deal crisper and more spirited than are the carefully rounded periods of the story-teller:

The old man glanced sternly at his son as he entered the room, and began:

'Your conduct, John, has given great pain both to your mother and myself. On the last occasion when I paid your college debts, I told you that you need never look to me for aid again – and I am determined to adhere to that resolution. What have you to say in extenuation of your conduct?'

'Well, sir,' said the young man, 'when a man has the misfortune to back the wrong horse in the St Leger, the Derby and the Oaks, he can hardly expect to have a balance on the right side. Everyone said that Zebra was a certain winner.'

'I can't conceive, John, where you get these low tastes from, and your judgement too is far from good. Are you not aware that Zebra comes on the mother's side from Bountiful, who always broke down at a crisis? I ought to know, for I lost two hundred pounds over the brute. Now who could look at the Racing Calendar and doubt that Carydon, who won, was a very dangerous horse. His granddam won the Cambridgeshire. Horse-racing is a degrading taste, however, and you must break yourself of it. What else have you spent your money on? There is a woman in the case, no doubt?'

'I am bound to confess, sir, that there is one young person to whom I have shown some attention.'

'Upon my word, I am astonished at your assurance. You appear to have no regard for the good name of the family. Who is this individual?'

'Fanny Davis is her name, sir, daughter of Old Molly Davis who keeps the tobacconist's shop.'

'What, you young rascal, you have taken up with the daughter of my old flame Molly! And how is she looking? Upon my word, I have half a mind to look in upon her when I come down to Cambridge to settle these debts of yours.'

Shorthand verbatim report:

'Too bad, John, too bad! Your mother thinks so as well as I. I said last time I'd never help you again. I won't either. What the devil have you to say for yourself? Hey?'

'Bad luck, sir.' (Pause) 'When a chap makes a mistake over the Leger, the Derby and the Oaks, he's bound to be hard hit. Zebra was reckoned a certainty.'

'These low tastes of yours, John. Can't imagine where you get 'em. No judgement either. Zebra's from Bountiful on the mother's side. She was always a faint-hearted one. I ought to know. Lost two hundred on the brute. Look at Carydon now! The Racing Calendar would tell you that she was dangerous. Granddam won the Cambridge. It's a degrading taste, horse-racing. You must drop it. What else have you been at? Some woman in tow, no doubt?'

'One little girl, sir.'

'Damn your impudence! You're a disgrace to your family. Who is she? Hey?'

'Fanny Davis. (Pause) Daughter of Old Molly at the Cigar shop.'

'What, you dog, Old Molly Davis' daughter! And how is Molly, hey? Gad, I'll look her up when I run down to settle your bills – hanged if I don't.'

And so on *ad infinitum*.

Our author has the best of it in literary finish and in grammar, but I am inclined to think that the shorthand reporter makes a more vivid narrative of it.

It is as impertinent as it is inartistic of a novelist to wander away from his story in order to give us his own opinions on this or that subject. George Eliot, Victor Hugo, Thackeray and Ouida are all somewhat addicted to it. What would we think of a play-writer who would suspend the acting of one of his pieces while he came upon the stage and discoursed to his audience about the positive philosophy, or the Euphrates Valley railway? Both the railway and the philosophy are excellent things in their place, and we are glad to hear something about them, but surely it would be well to ring down the curtain on the fifth act before holding forth upon them. So, no one could reasonably object to any gentleman unburdening himself of his opinions in an appendix, but to obtrude them upon us at a moment when we are trying to get into sympathy with his characters is to risk the spoiling of his story – as a story. It may become an excellent mosaic of philosophy, information, theology – pantology in fact – but it ceases to be a good novel.

But the moral, oh the moral! We don't want immoral stories but we want unmoral ones. Morals in a novel are as much out of place as physic in a champagne bottle. Why is vice always to be defeated and virtue triumphant? It is not so, I fear, in the world around us. Are we to be more prudish than Providence? There is not one of us who has not known in his experience of some good fellow who has gone to the wall, and of some scoundrel who has enjoyed every gift of fortune. It has jarred upon our finite sense of the fitness of things, but still the fact remained. Our instincts tell us that there ought to be some compensation which is beyond our ken, but we may be content to leave that question open and confine ourselves to depicting things as they are. Until we do so our romances are bound to be one-sided and unnatural.

It pleases us when that high-spirited and handsome youth, the hero, knocks the lumbering villain down. In real life, however, the scoundrel has a way of getting up again and returning the compliment. The heroine, too, has a miraculous trick of emerging pure and innocent at the end of the third volume after going through experiences which would, I fear, be too much for any poor lass who was only made of flesh and blood. The simple kind-hearted man of business does not invariably prosper. In this coarse, inartistic world of ours, he occasionally pays a shilling in the pound and dies in a lunatic asylum.[91] Such a denouement would however be 'in very questionable taste' – to quote one of the favourite insipidities of the British critic. We should, according to this enlightened band, draw the world not as it is, but as it ought to be – a principle which if applied to art would be productive of some startling effects. There would be an opening then for the painter of tender years who remarked that, though he had seen many sunsets, he had never seen anything which came up to his idea of what a sunset ought to be.

No, the touchstone of a novel is the interest. If it succeeds in absorbing our attention and taking us away from the work-a-day world around us, it may claim to be a good novel, but if it fails in this essential no amount of clever writing or originality of thought can make it anything but a failure. It may still be a remarkable book, and a most admirable piece of literary work, but from the moment when our sympathy with the characters relaxes it disqualifies itself from taking a high place among the romances. Judged by this standard, and by their power of riveting and retaining the interest of the reader from the first page to the last, I believe that the three finest novels of the century are from the same pen. *Foul Play*, *Hard Cash* and *It Is Never Too Late to Mend* are invariably the three dirtiest books in a circulating library – a very fair criterion of popular taste.[92] These three with *The Cloister and the Hearth*, Ouida's *Under Two Flags*, the latter part of Le Fanu's *Uncle Silas* and the first volume of Payn's *By Proxy* are as fine examples of pure storytelling as our literature can boast of.

I flatter myself that I am somewhat of a connoisseur of short stories. The wine-taster uses a liqueur glass, not a tumbler, and so the real flavour of an author can be appreciated best in his smaller productions. But how few there are who have written first-class tales. You could count them on your fingers. The reason is, I suppose, that when an author has hit upon a strong idea which may be amplified into a three-volume novel he cannot afford to throw it away upon a thirty-page story. Yet to my mind, the production of the short tales is the finer art of the two. Every little gem must be of the purest water and most delicately cut if it is to stand out among its fellows. There is no room for padding – every word must tell. It should be full of concentrated strength and yet flow easily and naturally. How distinct an art tale-writing is in its higher developments from novel-writing is shown by the fact that the masters of one have had no success at all at the other.[93] Poe, who has written two short tales of the very highest merit – 'The Gold-Bug' and 'The Murders of the Rue Morgue' – never even attempted a longer flight. Bret Harte, whose 'Luck of Roaring Camp' and 'Tennessee's Partner' are the very acme of pathos, fails to arouse any enthusiasm in the reader for *Gabriel Conroy*. Robert Louis Stevenson appears to be one of the few who are capable of producing a first-class tale and who can still excel in a more sustained effort. His 'Pavilion on the Links' is, to my mind, as certainly the best of recent tales as his *Dr Jekyll* is of the shilling dreadfuls. His manner and his matter are equally excellent.[94]

I don't know whether dogmatism is one of the symptoms of rheumatic gout. Looking over the last few pages, it looks as if I had been visited by an acute attack of it. Put it down to the abominable weather and the demoralising effect of this course of solitary confinement. I have been feeding on my own mind without taking in anything fresh, either by reading or talking, until there is a danger of my finding myself without an idea left to draw upon.

Some men don't keep any permanent stock of ideas but get them to order as they want them – and yet manage to pass as very well-informed and entertaining individuals. If a man crams himself in this way he should dole out his information very carefully and with great art, or he is liable to be detected. He must coax the conversation into his own channels – not drag it in. I remember an instance where the artifice was a little too transparent. I was returning from Kimberley with one Ferguson, a raw-boned ingenuous youth, and while passing through Capetown we were asked to dinner by an ex-premier of the Colony who had known my father. Ferguson, after his years of Bohemian life at the mines, was in the utmost trepidation at the idea of having to conform once more to the usages of civilised life. 'There'll be ladies there?' he asked. 'I'll have to take one down to dinner.' 'Probably,' I answered. 'In heaven's name,' he cried distractedly, 'what am I to talk to her about? I have no small talk. I know nothing about theatres or dress or any of the things which would interest a woman. I know nothing about anything except mines and niggers. I wish I was safely out of it.' 'My dear fellow,' said I, 'don't distress yourself. Look over any books you have and post yourself up in one or two subjects. A very little knowledge will enable you to pass as an agreeable companion.' Ferguson departed to his lodgings and, finding that the only book of information in his possession was a volume on the history of Ballooning, he studied this assiduously until he knew it from cover to cover. When the night of the dinner came round my companion appeared in most orthodox costume, and with all this accurate and unusual knowledge soaked well into his system. When we were waiting in the drawing room he informed us that a Jesuit named Francis Lana had first proposed to navigate the air by means of four hollow balls made of thin copper. As he descended the stairs with his lady I heard him assuring her that Black of Edinburgh had sent a bag of hydrogen into the air. When the soup was placed upon the table he told us how Joseph and Stephen Montgolfier had ascended in fire balloons at Annonay upon the 5th of June 1783. With the fish came a long account of how Madame Blanchard's balloon had taken fire and she herself been precipitated to the ground and killed, and how Lieutenant Harris and the younger Sadler met with a similar fate. The meat arrived but Ferguson still rambled on with his chosen subject. He told us how the great Nassau Balloon had started from Vauxhall Gardens and had after eighteen hours descended at Weilberg in the Duchy of Nassau. He also informed us that Nadar's great balloon contained no less that 215,363 cubic feet of gas and that it had taken as many as 35 soldiers into the air at one time. With the pastry he narrated the incidents of Mr Coxwell's ascent at Belfast in 1865 on which occasion the balloon became uncontrollable and many people were injured. Having rejoined the ladies he went on to tell with much spirit the story of the remarkable ascent made by Glaisher and Coxwell from Wolverhampton in 1863, on which occasion the great height of seven miles was reached, and the adventurers nearly lost their lives through the rarification of the atmosphere. At this point poor Ferguson exhausted his subject and suddenly dried up, nor could question or entreaty get another remark out of him for the remainder of the evening. However he had done enough to secure his reputation as a conversationalist. 'Your friend was brilliant, sir, brilliant,' our good host remarked to me as we parted. 'He is clearly a great aeronaut himself. We must see more of him – we really must.' It is as well he didn't, for within a week Jimmy Ferguson had forgotten all his suddenly acquired information and knew no more about balloons than he did about the differential calculus.

A man cannot bear all knowledge about in his head. Our little brain-attics have not got such very elastic walls, and there comes a time when, for everything fresh we learn, there is a chance of our forgetting something which we knew before. The new ideas elbow out the old ones. It becomes of the highest importance therefore that we should take nothing unnecessary into our brains and that we should docket and arrange all that we have so as to be able to use it to the best advantage at a moment's notice. In the first place there is a man's own profession or speciality. He should always study to have the latest and most accurate information upon that point, and no fact bearing upon it is too trivial to be remembered. Then there is his hobby. No human being should be complete without a hobby. It is to a man's real business as his shadow is to his person – always present and never obtrusive.[95] Be it literature or painting or gardening or pottery or music or whatever other of the endless varieties of hobbies, a man should be well up in it while keeping it strictly subordinate to the main business of his life. Then on other subjects, although a man cannot be expected to be equally well informed upon all, he should at least retain the keys of knowledge in his possession. He should know who are the authorities upon each point and what are the books which should be consulted. Thus an ordinary citizen is hardly expected to know much about Persian poetry and to have Hafiz, Firdousi and Ferideddin Attar at their fingers' ends, but he ought to know that Sir William Jones and the Baron von Hammer-Purgstall are great authorities upon the subject, and knowing that he can repair to his library and turn on the Persian tap at a moment's notice.[96] Similarly a man may be excused for not knowing very much about Buddhism – in spite of the fact that in its pure form it is infinitely the finest religion which the world has ever seen – but he really ought to know that St Hilaire[97] and Edwin Arnold are two writers who are always at hand to supply the deficiencies of his own knowledge. He does not wish to carry his property about wherever he goes. The grand thing is to be able to lay his hands upon it when he has a use for it.

Heigh ho! If my readers are as weary of the day as I am, they must be tired indeed. Oh for a stretch of the legs and a breath of fresh air, if there can be said to be any fresh air in this great asphyxiated city. The blind is down over the way and the easel stands out hard and clear against the lamp light like the fifth proposition of Euclid carved in wood.[98] The work is over for the day. Up above I hear the veteran stumbling about and dragging heavy objects about the floor. I have heard that from time to time he amuses himself by packing up his great campaigning trunk, as if there were some prospect of his being ordered away upon immediate foreign service. I can imagine his earnest grizzled face as he buckles and straps and fastens, stopping from time to time to decide as to whether this or that article will be wanted in the approaching campaign. Down below Herr Lehmann has ended his day's work and I hear the great piano closed down. Three white figures look in at my door and little treble voices wish me goodnight. 'Goodnight, my dears, goodnight.' The whole sleepy, blinking world is turning to rest, and so shall I.

CHAPTER 4

THE GOUT is leaving me. I feel it clearing slowly away like the mist from a mountain top. Fresh warm healthy blood is tingling in every vein. It is worth being ill to feel the glow of returning health. I am still weak and languid though – bad cess to the ailment which brought me so low. In the name of the great army of the gouty – of all the innumerable bulbous-toed battalions – I anathematise it with the great curse of the Bishop Ernulphus which embraces all curses which ever have been or which ever shall be.[99] Even the kind heart of my Uncle Toby could hardly object to my employing this tremendous weapon upon such an object.[100]

I was in such high spirits this morning that I set to work fixing up a little *jeu d'esprit* for Dr Julep. We had had one or two chats over the very different views taken of the British Pharmacopeia by various medical authorities, so I epitomised the fact in a quatrain:

Doctors agree that with potions and pills
You may readily cure the whole of life's ills
But each one, alas, has his different notions
As to what sort of pills and what sort of potions[101]

'When a man begins to chaff his medical attendant in doggerel verse,' remarked Dr Julep, 'it's a pretty sure sign of his convalescence.'

'I'll tell you what it is, Doctor,' said I reproachfully, 'I think you treated me in a very scurvy fashion in not coming to see me yesterday.'

'My dear sir,' he answered earnestly. 'It was my hospital day and I knew that you were going on all right.'

'It's not your prescription but your company I wanted,' said I frankly, 'so I shall insist upon having a double allowance of it today. I had a dreadfully lonely day yesterday. Your patients will be none the worse if you are ten minutes later in seeing them. Undo your coat, light a Manila, and try that armchair.'

'Thank you,' said he, smiling all over his little rosy face – as clear and as healthy as a Ribston pippin[102] – 'I won't smoke, but I will break my journey here with all the pleasure imaginable.'

'I've got a problem for you this morning,' I remarked as he settled down in his chair. 'My sleep is not very good while I am confined to the house and I think of some strange things during the night. This is something in your line, so I thought I would submit it to you.'

'Let us have it,' he said in the half-amused, condescending voice which medicos usually adopt towards laymen when they find them in an inquisitive humour.

'You will agree,' said I, 'that the majority of deaths in this world are from maladies which have been contracted by infection, or from exposure to the weather or from unhealthy living, or from some hereditary taint in the constitution.'

'I can hardly imagine any death except from violence or from old age which does not come from one or other of these causes,' he answered.

'Very well. Then death from old age really means, I suppose, that there comes a time when the sum total of all the worries and cares and duties and pleasures of life is too much for our bodily machinery, and wears it out.'

'Quite so.'

'Now supposing a mortal who had no possible hereditary weakness – who came from a perfectly sound stock – was placed in such circumstances that he could neither catch infection or incur disease in any possible manner, what would happen then?'

'Why, if such immunity was possible, and if you could protect a man against every noxious influence,' said Dr Julep, stroking his chin meditatively, 'I suppose he would have to die of old age.'

'But if you were also able to remove all trouble from his life,' I persisted, 'if you were to manage that he should have no care, no anxiety, no emotion – that all should be smooth and easy for him – how long would it be before old age would overtake him?'

'I don't quite see how you are going to do all this,' said Dr Julep.

'But I do. I have thought it out to the smallest details. The first point in the experiment is to select a perfectly healthy subject. I should choose a young country lad whose grandfathers and grandmothers on each side were still hearty. I should shut this lad up in a building specially adapted for his residence, and erected in some eminently healthy locality. In this building there should be several large airy rooms for his use and a long corridor for active exercise. All air passing into the house, however, would be strained through antiseptic air filters – I believe there are such contrivances' – the Doctor nodded – 'so that there should be no possibility of any noxious germ contaminating the atmosphere. In this way he would be absolutely fenced in from all infection. His water and food should be purified in a similar fashion, and his diet should be most carefully regulated and attention paid to the time occupied at his meals, and the thorough mastication of his food. He should have certain hours allotted for work, for exercise, for amusement and for sleep – with occasional modifications to prevent the routine from becoming intolerably monotonous. The atmosphere of the whole house should by an arrangement of hot water pipes be kept at a constant temperature, and the drainage should be most carefully looked after. Now I want to know how long that man is going to live, and what is going to kill him.'

'Why, he would get along very nicely for seventy years or so,' said my companion, 'and then his machinery would run down and he would come to a stop.'

'Would it, though?' I argued. 'The man has had no emotions or troubles or necessity for struggling for his living or pleasures, which take it out of our vitality more even than work does. I believe he would live for twice seventy years and be a hale man at the end of it.'

'And I believe the chances are that he would go melancholy mad, or that you would find the hall door of your model dwelling open some fine morning and that your prisoner had wandered off to breathe some less restrained, if more poisonous, atmosphere.'

'It's a very pretty little problem all the same,' said I stoutly. 'You put it into my head by your remarks the other day about the coming millennium when all disease is to be abolished by inoculation.'

'That I firmly believe in,' the Doctor answered, 'that is, if the type of disease remains the same. You know that the type of disease is a thing which is continually changing. Ailments which were common a few centuries ago are never heard of now, and others which are only too familiar now would, in the natural course of things, be extinct before very long even if Science did not give them a "coup-de-grâce." In this stage of the world's development we don't get the plague, or the sweating sickness, or the black death, any more than a middle-aged man usually gets the thrush or mumps or the whooping-cough. The race has had it and is fortified against a second attack. Where do the new diseases come from? Ah, we can't answer that question. They are new emanations from the foul ocean of morbid possibilities.'

'Perhaps you think that the type of disease alters with some subtle modification of the human type?'

'That is very possible,' he remarked. 'The human race has certainly not reached the zenith of its development. In a myriad years it will probably have so altered that to compare a body of that day with a body of this would be like comparing an educated Englishman with a chimpanzee. Even during the few thousands of years of which we have any knowledge there has been a change in our outside husks, which, though small compared to the change in our minds, is still sufficiently well marked. Old man had more bone in his skull and less brain, better marked ridges above his eyebrows, better hair, a black complexion and prominent canine teeth.'

'And what do you think is the direction of future change?' I asked.

'Why, Darwin – peace be with him! – says that our descendants are to be hairless and toothless. You can't count the number of dentists' brass plates in an eligible thoroughfare, or look down from the circle onto the heads of the young men in the stalls, without seeing that both these appendages of ours are in a very bad way indeed. I'm sometimes inclined to think that there are two types in process of formation – the man with the big brain and no muscle, and the man with the great muscle and no brain. The fact is that our individual lives are so very short compared with the great periods over which these changes extend, that we can form very little conception of what is coming. A few seconds are a longer fraction of a day than a life of eighty years is of the time during which we know that this world has been in existence. If a man lived for only a few seconds of daylight, and his son the same, and his for a hundred generations, what would their collective experience tell them of the phenomenon which we call night? So all our history and knowledge is no guarantee that our world is not destined in the future for experiences of which we can form no conception. It is not safe for us to be dogmatic upon such a matter. If man, as we know him, is a lineal descendant of the sea-urchins, who shall say what may be at the other end of the chain.'

'An echinus at one end and a demigod at the other,' I suggested. 'The great series starts from pure matter and works its way upwards, shedding off a little of its grossness at every stage until it develops into unalloyed spirituality. But while I can understand that we are working up towards some glorious destination, I am still in doubt as to what function is assigned to the individual soul, and what becomes of it after its separation from the body – if indeed it is capable of having any existence apart from the body.'

'It is a means to an end,' remarked my companion. 'What becomes of the little grey seed when the stem has sprouted and the flower unfolded?'

'You mean,' said I, 'that what we call our souls are of no value of themselves, but are only the index which shows how far we have got in spiritual development.'

'Quite so,' said the Doctor complacently. 'At any time of the world's history you might take an average of people's souls which would show you the level attained at that date by the human family in spirituality, refinement and virtue. This average soul has on the whole, with a few short relapses, gone on steadily rising from generation to generation, and will, I believe, continue to do so until it arrives at absolute perfection. Good is rising and evil is sinking, just as you see oil and water mixed in a bottle clearing off and forming a layer the one over the other. What will happen when the race becomes all-good – whether it will then be taken into partnership by the great source of all things, as an apprentice who has worked his way industriously is occasionally admitted into the Firm, or whether good and God may prove to be synonymous, are problems which there is no prospect of our being able to answer. You remember Seneca's fine saying: "The good man differs from God in nothing but duration."'

'If I wasn't a cripple I'd get up to shake hands with you, Doctor,' said I. 'You've expressed my own ideas, with a few variations, far more clearly than I could have done myself. I feel that we do not take a broad enough or hopeful enough view of creation and the creator. The insanity of the idea that a man will be judged upon his own individual merits or demerits, when not only his tendency to evil but also the weakness of mind which forbids him to combat that tendency are as much hereditary and part of his nature as the colour of his hair, has always seemed to me to be past all description. No, I do firmly believe that we are *all* making for a common goal, and that we will reach it, every man of us, at some appointed time. The higher natures will get there quickest, but sooner or later not one of us shall fail to be there.'

'But not just yet awhile,' said Dr Julep with a twinkle of the eyes, jumping up and putting on his hat. 'Things jog along in their own way *ohne hast und ohne rast*.[103] It will be a terrible long time yet before the world is ripe. Even death won't teach us anything, but will only set us working under fresh guises and in new combinations, until the great consummation comes. And however we work or in whatever form we contribute to this all-important end, we are equally fulfilling a lofty mission. If in the lapse of years and the

endless change of matter our molecules, or some of them, helped
to form a door handle or an earthenware pot, we are none the
less playing as dignified a part in the great scheme as now. All
works to the one end. There is no small and there is no great in
nature. The breaking of a pane of glass is as important an event
in the working-out of the all-comprehensive problem, as is the
death of a man. And now, my dear friend, I must positively run
away from you and your dangerously fascinating problems. No
imprudence, remember: plain living, no wine, perfect rest and
regular medicine. Don't imagine that you are quite out of the
woods yet. Adieu!'

Adieu, my cheery little physician, adieu! I declare when I hear a
man put forward views which are not founded upon the idea that
the Divine being is a Moloch or a fiend, my very soul leaps within
me. I feel as though he had brought a whiff of bracing air into the
room with him. The inane doctrine of fearing the source of all
good, and of loving what we cannot comprehend, is a great stifling
nightmare which has weighed us all down too long. All things are
being woven into one beautiful harmonious pattern, and though
we see so small a section of it that we cannot comprehend the
symmetry of the whole vast design, yet the day will come when it
will be completed and when we may appreciate it, and understand
how we have contributed towards it. Perhaps evil and sin and pain
may prove to be merely the dark background which is necessary
to make the bright design stand out hard and clear.

Death is an ugly word, but from my experience – and I have
seen many deathbeds – it is not usually a very painful process. In
many cases a man dies without having incurred during the whole
of his fatal illness as much actual pain as would have arisen from
a whitlow[104] or an abscess of the jaw. And it is just those deaths
which seem most terrible to the onlooker which are the least so
to the actual sufferer. When a man is overtaken by an express
and shivered into fragments, or when he falls from a fourth floor
window and is dashed into a jelly, the unfortunate spectators are
convulsed with horror. Yet it is very doubtful if the deceased,
could he return to life, would be able to remember anything at

all about the transaction. There are a few complaints, notably cancer and some abdominal ailments, which cause considerable pain before proving mortal; but the various fevers, apoplexy, blood poisonings of every variety, lung diseases and in fact the great majority of serious maladies are not commonly characterised by much suffering. I remember some thirty years ago passing through the wards of the Royal Edinburgh Infirmary[105] and seeing the actual cautery applied in a case of spinal disease. The white hot iron was pressed firmly into the patient's back, without any anaesthetic being used to deaden the pain, and what with the terrible sight and the nauseating smell of burned flesh, I felt sick and faint. Yet to my astonishment the patient never flinched or moved a muscle of his face, and on my enquiring afterwards he informed me that the proceeding was absolutely painless, a remark which was corroborated by the operating surgeon. 'The nerves are so completely and instantaneously destroyed,' he explained, 'that they have no time to convey a painful impression.' I have often thought since then that many other things in nature which appear to us to be very harsh and cruel, might perhaps take quite another complexion if we had the testimony of the people principally concerned. David Livingstone, lying torn and mangled under the claws of the lion, must have been a horror-inspiring spectacle, and yet he has left it on record that his own sensations were pleasurable rather than otherwise. I am very sure that if the newly born infant and the man who had just died could compare their experiences, the former would have proved to be the greatest sufferer. It is not for nothing that the first thing that the newcomer into this planet does is to open its toothless mouth and protest energetically against the decrees of fate.

'There is nothing small in Nature and there is nothing great,' says Julep. It sounds a little paradoxical, but when I come to look into it I can see exactly what he is driving at. He means, I take it, that every tiniest as well as every largest thing is working to one end, each in its own place, and that that end is of such enormous majesty and importance as to render everything else subordinate and insignificant. The small things which we might be tempted to look upon as ludicrous or unsavoury are of as much intrinsic importance as the weightiest which the human mind can conceive. The slime left by a snail upon a gravel path has as definite a function in the scheme of creation as has the Milky Way, and the cuttings of a man's nails are as much part of Nature's stock in trade and as necessary for the correct working out of her calculations as are Jupiter and all his moons. The little screws look very insignificant beside the big piston, but if you removed all your screws where would your engine be then?

I daresay if we only knew a little more about the matter we would find that the large things in Nature are arranged on exactly the same lines and under the same laws as what we presume to call the small ones. For example, that the millions of heavenly bodies have taken up exactly the same positions in the firmament which as many grains of sand would do if they were removed from the action of gravitation and allowed to arrange themselves *in vacuo*. I remember once looking through a microscope at the crystals of snow, and shortly afterwards through a telescope at those nebulae which according to some astronomers are the raw material of the worlds of the future. In the infinitesimally small ice-spicules, and in the indescribably vast masses of vapour, there was a marvellous coincidence of shape. Nature had built them on the same design but on different scales. Look at what is called the dumb-bell nebula, and then at the feathery snow crystals, and then, if you have the chance, at the ultimate fibrils which form your own muscles, and you will see how fond Nature is of repeating her patterns, and what a wonderful uniformity there is running through all creation.

Good Mrs Rundle, the lodging-house keeper, came up to lay my luncheon and is glad to see me so much better. I think I have mentioned that she is a widow handicapped in the race of life by three children. It is no wonder, poor soul, if her face is a little hard and so puckered up with wrinkles that it looks as though her skin had been made for a larger woman, and she had been compelled to take in tucks in it. Every one of those lines is a record of some fresh trial. Evil fate has scratched its memoranda all over her face as Robinson Crusoe cut the days and weeks into the post. If we could read that grim register we should perhaps be inclined to smile at the petty things which can have such an effect on a human being. Genuine griefs there have been, no doubt. The face in her portrait downstairs taken ten years ago is as smooth as a child's, and the sudden death of her life-partner was the beginning of those ominous lines. When once, however, Destiny takes to chalking things up, it is astonishing how quickly the score runs up, and what small worries may add to it. That little line beneath the eye dates from the day when the very eligible young tenant disappeared at the end of his month and left behind him a dilapidated hair-trunk containing a sewer grating, half a dozen bricks, and a fifty-six pound weight. That other one beside it made *its* appearance when little Mary caught the scarlatina and the first-floor front, who had been reckoned upon as a fixture, moved out at once for fear of infection. There is one little scratch for the rise in coals, and another to mark the day when the Major fell down the back stairs, and another which dates from the time when my predecessor in the second floor announced his intention of departing forthwith unless one of Johann Lehman's pupils would cease worrying an unfortunate violin, whose frightful screams and wails had aroused the compassion of the whole neighbourhood. What a catalogue of little miseries, all of them real enough and grave enough to her at the time, are chronicled in that mesh work of wrinkles. The *peine forte et dure*[106] of daily life has crushed all the soul out of her. Poor dumb inarticulate creature, from her anxious joyless eyes to the ends of her worn and distorted fingers she is a walking protest against the thought that this life is anything but a fleeting and transient stage which leads to something higher. If this existence were to prove to be the be-all and end-all with her, then Creation would be nothing more than a grim joke upon the part of the Creator.

Strange how women love to talk of what has been saddest in their lives. Even in the lowest orders a man usually keeps his past griefs to himself while a woman cackles them forth to anyone who will listen to her. When a wound has skinned over, a not unpleasant titillation is caused by touching it, and so perhaps they derive some mental satisfaction from dwelling on the memory of former misfortune. The one great blow which Mrs Rundle has had in her life was the sudden death of her husband, and yet she cannot lay the cloth for my luncheon without pouring every detail of the matter into my ears.

'Which we'd had words in the morning,' said she, 'and he slammed the door that hard that he brought down the terrar-cottar statuette beside the hatstand which I'd given two and threepence to an Italian for only the week before. It was a beautiful statuette, and after the funeral Mr Mason the decorator round the corner had it joined together as good as new, only that he put the left arm wrong side foremost which gave it a kind of constrained and twistified sort of attitude. I has just a-finished the laying of the dinner when Mr Browning of the firm comes driving to the door in a growler.[107] "Your husband's very ill, Mrs Rundle," says he. "I think you has best come back with me," says he. Lor' it's all like a dream after that, or as if I'd read it in a book, the gentleman's grave kind face, and the long drive with the rattling of the wheels and the jingling of the windows! Then the narrow door, and the stone steps and the little office, and someone saying "Better not let her up!" They tried to hold me back but I broke through them and there he was, lying on three chairs cold and stiff with a handkerchief over his face and his waistcoat all unbuttoned. I felt real ashamed that he hadn't a cleaner shirt on, with all those gentlemen looking. We were taken back together – I don't rightly remember how, and they laid him out in the back room, but they put him in a draught between the door and the window, so when they were all gone I moved him into his own corner. It wasn't till I went into the parlour and saw the plate laid for him and his knife and fork and beer jug, and the long cherry-wood pipe[108] standing ready by the side of the fire, that it came home to me that the poor dear was really gone and that I should never hear his voice again. Ah, sir, he was a dear good husband to me and I haven't a word to say against him – though he did break the terrar-cottar statuette.'

The poor soul has evidently got the two calamities so coupled in her mind that she cannot discuss the one without conjuring up the other. That thought of hers too about the dirty shirt when she saw her husband lying dead was characteristic and distinctive. It was not heartlessness, but merely want of imagination. Her mind would not rise to the conception of death, but the soiled linen was well within its range and made an instant appeal to it. It's the fine dust of daily petty worries and troubles which plays the deuce with the delicate human machine. We may rouse our souls to some supreme effort, but we cannot steel them against the slow sapping of a sordid commonplace existence. Joan of Arc or Charlotte Corday would soon lose their heroism if condemned to keep a boarding house.[109]

There have been theological difficulties downstairs. Dicky and Tommy have been bringing their infantine doubts to their mother who responded – after the fashion of very august ecclesiastical assemblies – by rapping them upon the head with a thimble and threatening to send them to bed. Dicky, who has had a book on natural history with coloured plates presented to him, wants to know what the carnivorous animals lived upon while they were in the Ark. Mary, the little girl, suggested potted meat and was met by wild derision from the two small Colensos.[110] Tommy wants to know who Adam and Eve's children married. Susan the scullery maid, who goes to the Sunday school, suggested Potiphar's wife and then explained that she was thinking of something else, while the cook's contribution to the debate was the remark that 'she never seed what things was coming to!' Finally the whole question was referred to the second-floor lodger – raised to a higher level, as they say in Parliament – but the wily invalid refused to commit himself. The only practical outcome of the discussion was a resolution supported by landlady, lodger, cook and housemaid that children should be seen and not heard, with an addendum that children should never talk about what they don't understand – a maxim which, if universally applied, would rather limit the field of human conversation.

It is all very well to treat this matter lightly but there is a graver side to it as well. The little episode is typical of a process which is going on in every land and has been in every time. It is the

moulding of the natural into the conventional – the stamping out
of the free healthy impulses of the human mind. A steady pressure
is brought to bear upon the child's bump of enquiry[111] until it is
quite atrophied away and the mind left mutilated for life. There
are very very few who can resist this insidious process, which
robs a man of his individuality almost before he knows that he
has an individuality to lose. Those two little youngsters in twenty
years' time would probably be honestly shocked to hear anyone
propounding the questions which they are asking now, and yet
they will be as far away from finding an answer to them. Their
present frame of enquiry is a more healthy one than their eventual
state of satisfied ignorance. Mother's teaching is at the root of all
the conservatism of the world – and every budding intellect has
a natural bias towards radicalism and free thought. Woman's
influence is the brake which is perpetually keeping the human
coach from thundering away too precipitately down the road of
progress. I know that if I were a leader of the Tory Party I would
hurry up the question of female suffrage, for of every million of the
new electors nine hundred and fifty thousand would be reactionists
to the backbone.[112] Did you ever know a woman who was of the
opinion that Cromwell may have had some justification for cutting
off his good-looking sovereign's head? The feelings of the sex set
in favour of right divine, unquestioning obedience, implicit faith,
and mediaevalism generally – and their influence upon the young
generation is the strongest influence upon this earth.

Talking of Charles and his lost cause, it is strange how in this
world you will invariably get a body of men to support any idea
or doctrine, however absurd or grotesque it may be. No doubt
there are thousands living in England now who consider that the
Stewarts[113] were a most ill-used and persecuted family and that they
were shamefully treated by an ungrateful country. Joe Smith with
his tablets of beaten gold,[114] or the missing heir with his budget of
palpable lies,[115] have no difficulty in arousing enthusiasm among
great crowds of followers. If a man were to stump the country
and announce that the moon really was a green cheese – caused
by the gradual caseation of the Milky Way – he would soon find

himself the leader of a new school of thought. There actually is an imbecile in existence who asserts that the earth is flat and who has persuaded many people to adopt his views.[116] As long as there are two sides to a question, so long you will find staunch minorities who attach themselves to obsolete or unpopular opinions. Why, even Cain has had his apologists. Schlegel[117] narrates that the Cainites were a powerful body in Central Asia and that a relic of them is still found among the Ishudes, who tell the story of the first murder with a strong party bias, representing Abel as a mean pitiful fellow who richly deserved his fate. No man is too stupid or too wicked not to have a following. It is an exemplification of the clever French aphorism *Un sot trouve toujours un plus sot qui l'admire*.[118]

Miss Oliver sits in the window opposite with her back turned to the street so that the light may fall full upon her easel. If she could only put upon canvas her own graceful dark-clad figure and the rich coil of her bronze-coloured hair showing up against the ivory whiteness of her neck, she would produce a picture worthy of the Salon. It is a pleasure to me to watch those busy fingers working away so energetically and to think that I am the unknown motive power which has set them going. She has come to the third little daub now, as I reckon, and will have finished by nightfall. Two days' work for a guinea is not very much, but I have no doubt, poor lass, that she is in high feather about it. I shall look up some of my friends when I get about and see if I cannot persuade them to give her an order for a few of her studies from nature.

Why is it that mediocrity has such an affection for nature? I confess that I can't see where all this admiration comes in. When one sees a group of tourists at Chamonix or the Righi open-mouthed and wonder-eyed,[119] protesting to each other that the great masses of stone and of congealed water in front of them have had an elevating effect upon their mind, one cannot but marvel at the minds which could be elevated by such means. An elevation of the earth or a depression in it, an accumulation of water in a hollow or the falling of it over a ledge, are all pleasant to an eye accustomed to a uniform landscape and the monotony of city streets, but beyond this merit of variety what is there to recommend it? The human mind should be so enormously superior to, and so infinitely grander than, any mere earthly phenomenon, that it degrades itself and loses its true position whenever it professes to be awestruck or subdued by any combination of matter. There is, I freely own, a fit and proper reverence due to all created things, as being dim reflections of the Creator, but the mind, being the highest and noblest of all his works, must ever be held far above the whole united firmament. Nature is a marvellous thing but not so marvellous as your own entity. Beware of the soul becoming a flunkey where it should be a master. What is size and time and distance to the ethereal elastic spirit which dwells within us? Chateaubriand and Co. have raved about the 'soul-subduing' wonders of Niagara – 700 yards of river falling over 150 feet of rock – but in virtue of my superiority I can lie upon this sofa and can conjure up the image of a fall which shall extend from horizon to horizon, and the summit of which shall be higher than the eye can reach, and eternally veiled by its own curtain of spray. Instead of Niagara dwarfing the human mind, the human mind can very readily dwarf Niagara. Mount Everest you say is seven and twenty thousand feet in height, but my mind can evolve clearly the image of a gigantic peak which shoots its snow-clad crest to the very verge of our terrestrial atmosphere. What if the planet Uranus is 1,800,000,000 miles from us, in the twinkling of an eye my fancy can transplant me past it, and I find myself gazing out at the unknown void beyond, and back at our own sun which shines dimly in the remotest distance. There are only two thoughts which the human intelligence cannot attain – eternity and infinitude.[120] At all else, from the spores of a sea weed to the grouping of the constellations, it can look down with the intelligent superiority of one, who if not absolute owner, is at least tenant in possession. The attitude of the man of the future towards his surroundings will not be one of wonder and debasement, but rather of high-handed command. We have not realised yet our own towering position in the Universe, or how absolutely all things inanimate are subordinate to us. There will prove to be a deep meaning in the conception of a faith which is capable of transplanting the mountains. Our souls, even during life, may perhaps refuse to be fettered to this petty globe, and may make excursions into its own outlying dominions beyond the uttermost stars. The uncontested phenomena of clairvoyance and of modern spiritualism,[121] and the inexplicable powers possessed by the higher esoteric Buddhists,[122] are small straws which show the set of the current of coming progress. What says the wise Emerson? 'A correspondent revolution in things will attend the influx of the spirit. The kingdom of man over nature he shall enter without more wonder than the blind man feels who is gradually restored to perfect sight.'[123]

Who should come in after luncheon but my good neighbour from above – clad in a somewhat rusty tweed suit, but retaining the peculiar slinging gait and easy lounge of his class. 'Should have been in yesterday,' said he heartily, 'but I was busy packing my traps together in case of an emergency. I'm all right now,' he added with a sigh of relief. 'I could start at a couple of hours notice.'

'Start!' I exclaimed. 'Why, Major, you don't mean seriously to say that your services may be required in the field?'

'And why not, sir – why not?' asked my companion hotly. 'Do you imagine, sir, that my age disqualifies me?'

'Your health,' I suggested.

'My health is never so good as when I am in harness. A campaign acts upon me as a cholagogue, sir – stirs my liver up. Podophyllin is nothing to it. Why, I assure you, I started for Magdala weighing nine stone eight and as yellow as a guinea, and I came back as brown as a chip, and turned the scales at eleven stone. That's what a campaign did for me, sir.'

'But I had no idea—' said I a little timidly, for the Veteran was evidently very touchy upon the question of his fitness for hard work. 'I had no idea that there were any complications between our government and foreign powers. I was under the impression that we were at peace with the whole world.'

The Major produced a folded newspaper from his coat-tail pocket and after much fumbling and searching pounced upon a very small telegram in diminutive type which was stowed away under the meteorological chart in a back column. Crumpling the paper up so as to bring this item to the front, he inflated his chest and smiled at me with a smile of superior knowledge. 'At peace with the world,' said he impressively, 'listen to this. "The Russian governor of Kashgaria has determined to send a brigade of Cossacks to the Kuldja frontier in order to check the depredations of the marauding Tartars." There, what do you think of that!' roared the Major, slapping the paper down upon the table. 'When telegrams like that appear in the public press it is time for officers of the reserve to pack their boxes.'

'Dear me!' said I. 'I am a most wretched hand at geography. I sometimes mix up the very places that I have visited. Kuldja, I presume, is upon the Indian frontier?'

'Nothing of the kind, sir,' the Major answered sternly. 'It is a thousand miles or more from our Indian possessions. Kuldja is an outlying province in the north of China. We are not to be hoodwinked with all this nonsense about Tartar marauders. No, sir, the Russian bear wants to fasten its greedy claws upon Kuldja itself. I say that it is time for Great Britain to put her foot down and to declare once for all that she will not suffer it.'

'But I understand you to say that Kuldja belongs to China and not to England. I don't observe in this paper that China has shown any particular alarm about this Russian advance.'

'And is an Englishman to take the initiative from a Chinaman?' asked the Major with withering sarcasm. 'Gad, sir, we may have deteriorated but we have not quite come down to that yet. If the Chinese Empire has not spirit enough to defend its own frontier, is that any reason why we should allow the Russians to strengthen their base in Central Asia?'

'What are we to do then, Major?' I asked.

'Do!' he cried, with his grizzly whiskers bristling with indignation. 'We must put down this infamous land-hunger. If need be, we must take Kuldja ourselves and hold it against all comers. We must blockade the Black Sea, send an ironclad squadron into the Baltic, batter down the forts at Kronstadt and set St Petersburg in a blaze. We must have our cruisers in the White Sea and reduce Archangel to ashes, while our Pacific squadron sinks or captures every Russian warship in those waters. At the same time we must buy over the Amir of Afghanistan and push a couple of hundred thousand Anglo-Indian troops through the passes of the Hindoo-Koosh. If necessary I would arm every male in the country from twenty to fifty and pack them off to Asia. That's my idea of a spirited policy, which would check aggressiveness. By Heavens, I'd make them rue the day that ever they laid hands upon Kuldja!'

I suppose that every country is afflicted with ultra-patriots of this explosive type. Jingoism, Chauvinism, Panslavism, Spread-eagleism, it breaks out in nasty blotches all over the globe, and a very unhealthy irritative condition it is. The only thing to be said for it is that it is a shade or two better than the sordid preference of private to public interests which prevails in some other quarters. Here is this old gentleman, who is a kind-hearted man enough – I saw him throw a beetle out of the window rather than crush it – howling out for a war which would put a third of the world into mourning, and all for the sake of some grievance which is so shadowy that it rests upon the supposition of a supposition. What makes him more dangerous is that he is in deadly earnest over it – so earnest that he is quite ready and even eager to risk his own life upon the quarrel. Imagine the danger of an autocratic system of government by which such a man as this might find himself at the head of a state with unrestrained powers of pursuing what he would call a spirited policy towards his neighbours.

While these thoughts were passing through my head the Major was standing upon my tigerskin with his back to the fireplace, red and angry like a smouldering volcano, with a thick wreath of cigar smoke curling up from his crater. It may have been the influence of the narcotic or it may have been the effect of my smiling and pacific visage, but the warlike cloud cleared gradually away from his rubicund features and left him benign and cheerful.

'I am going up to the Horse Guards with my invention this

afternoon,' he remarked. 'I have some hope that they will adopt my idea of a metallic gunstock.'

'I had no idea that you were an inventor, Major,' said I.

'Yes, worse luck! I wouldn't be living up two pair of stairs in an attic if it wasn't for that same turn for invention. It has certainly elevated me in the world. I assure you what I have spent in patents would have been enough to keep me in luxury for my old age. The vexation of the thing is that these plans and contrivances of mine, the fruit of a life's experience and of more money than I could afford, are rotting away in the drawers or pigeon-holes of some deputy-assistant nobody at the War Office who has just brains enough to sign his name at the back of the quarterly cheque which represents his own unearned and exorbitant salary. So is it not a disgrace?' cried the Major, waxing warm again. 'Is it not an insufferable scandal? Here is England, the richest country in the world, and the one in which mechanical and inventive genius has reached its highest development – and yet, thanks to our effete administration, we must be for ever the last to adopt an improvement not only in military but – to our shame be it said! – in naval matters also. Who brought out the propeller? A Swede – who, after offering it in vain to the British Admiralty, took his invention over to America with him. Who brought out ironclads? The French. Monitors? The Americans. Rams? The Americans. Breech-loaders? The Prussians. Machine guns? The French. Torpedoes? The Americans. How is it that we are nowhere in the list? Is it want of money or want of brains or want of individual enterprise? Nothing of the kind. It's because we have a set of infernal lazy rascals at the head of affairs who have been pitchforked into their position by some titled relation and who don't care a brass farthing about the credit of the nation as long as they are allowed to have a good time – to guzzle at public dinners and to return thanks when some sycophant proposes their health. Their health indeed! By Jove, I would hang one or two of them if I had my way! Why should the humble private soldier be liable to death for dereliction of duty, while the superiors of his superiors openly and notoriously neglect theirs? If our rank and file were as much behind Continental troops as our departmental officials and administrators are behind those of foreign countries, I wouldn't give much for Bank of England stock.'[124]

'You speak feelingly on the subject,' I remarked.

'So would you if you had had my experience,' said he. 'Is there a man who doubts that if the business of a private firm was managed in the same way as is the public business of the country, that firm would speedily find itself in the Bankruptcy Court? It is not the soldier or the sailor or the dockyard man who is overpaid. The mischief lies with the sinecurists, the useless chiefs of useless departments with heads as wooden as the desks they write upon – the favoured young scions of the aristocracy who lounge into their offices at their own sweet will, and spend their days in retailing and inventing questionable anecdotes. Those are the red-tape worms who would have sapped England's strength if she were not the robust elastic country that she is. I'll look in tomorrow and show you one or two of my models and plans – if it won't bore you. You appear to take an intelligent interest in the matter.'

That's what Dr Julep remarked about his germ theories and his beneficent attempts to prolong human life, I reflected. Strange that my mind should be attracted by two subjects which are so exactly the converse of each other. Perhaps, however, they all fit in this wonderful conundrum of life and have each their subordinate but indispensable part in the grand scheme of Creation. Slaying and saving, breaking down and building up, dissolving and reuniting, synthesis and analysis; who shall say which is ultimately the true philanthropy and which the violation of Nature's profound and mysterious laws?

CHAPTER 5

I HAVE HAD a very momentous experience this morning – so moving a one that I rose superior to my ankle joint and forgot all about my rheumatic gout. This was nothing less than a visit from a young lady. Not a very rare event, perhaps, in the eyes of the lucky dogs who have had the good sense to stick to conventionality and to cultivate society,[125] but to a deserted friendless womanless old wanderer like me it was a portentous occurrence indeed. For a moment a wild hope rose up in my heart that there existed a real living woman who had come to claim kinship with me, or at least to show some interest in me were it only on the strength of knowing those whom I had known. No one values women so much as the man who has had to do without them.[126]

She was shown in immediately after breakfast, well-gloved, dark-dressed, thickly veiled, with a square brown paper package in her hands. I sprang off the sofa and, bowing her into a chair, sat palpitating in front of her, combating against all manner of wild impulses which urged me to ring for wine or coffee and bread-and-butter.

'You probably don't know me by sight,' she said, throwing up her veil and revealing the pale interesting features of my neighbour over the way.

'Oh yes, I know you very well indeed,' I answered frankly. 'I have frequently had the pleasure of seeing you at the window.'

She smiled and a faint colour tinged her white cheeks. 'I sit in the window in order to get light enough for my work,' she said, speaking in the deep rich voice which is the only physical mark of good breeding which I have never met with among the under-bred.

'I have taken the liberty of calling upon you to thank you for your extreme kindness in favouring me with a commission, and to learn whether the sketches are satisfactory.'

'But, my dear young lady,' said I, 'there must be some mistake. Did not Mrs—'

'Your delicacy has been as great as your generosity,' she interrupted smiling. 'Mrs Rundle gave her instructions admirably, but when I came over last night to know whether the subjects were to her taste, she was compelled to acknowledge whom the pictures really belonged to.'

'I generally employ an agent in these matters,' I explained, feeling rather hot and uncomfortable, as if my hair needed brushing down behind. 'It is the usual custom. May I ask if these are the sketches?' I continued, pointing at the brown paper parcel.

'I have them here,' she said, undoing the string with tremulous fingers. 'I do hope that you will like them. This first one is a picture of a Cornish pilchard boat.'

'Very nice indeed,' said I critically.

'And this represents the Dieppe fishing fleet going out at night, and this is their return next day, with all the men's wives waiting upon the quay.'

'Capital!' I cried, with a wooden smile. 'By the way, what an extraordinary existence a fisherman's wife must lead. She appears to be invariably standing at the extreme edge of the quay with her hand shading her eyes, and her gaze fixed upon the horizon.'

My visitor looked at me with a troubled and somewhat annoyed expression. It is dangerous to venture upon what is usually termed dry humour with women unless you know them very well. In the latter case they put it down as harmless idiocy, but until they have learned to know your ways, it invariably puzzles and offends them.

'This last one,' she said, ignoring my attempt at jocularity, 'represents the hauling up of the nets when there has been a heavy catch. I am very fond of the sea, and my father always says that my sea pictures are better than any of my other sketches. I hope you don't think the subjects too uniform!'

What a heaven's blessing it is that we can still keep our private opinions locked away at the very bottom of our souls. These attempts at thought-reading which we hear of should be made a criminal offence. Why, if such a system became universal, life would soon be unbearable.[127] Now for all this world could give, I would not have that anxious wistful-eyed creature suspect the aversion which I have for the class of sketches which she has selected. I ranged the four of them upon my table, therefore, and stood in front of them with my head cocked upon one side, beaming at them with as much admiration as Ruskin in front of his Vittore Carpaccio. What an insufferable and immoral creature a rigidly truthful mortal would be!

'But surely,' said she, looking round my room, 'you cannot think of hanging my crude pictures among these beautiful paintings. If I had seen your room or known what taste you have, I should never have dared to draw anything for you. Why – whatever can have induced you to order daubs like this when you were surrounded by so many masterpieces?'

'Speculation,' I said boldly: 'no one can tell how valuable these may become someday when you have made your name, perhaps, and developed into a Miss Thompson or a Rosa Bonheur.[128] A great deal of money has been made by far-sighted people in that way. I am so well satisfied with the results of my investment that I should consider it a favour if you will paint me a larger and more ambitious picture.'

'It is so very kind and good of you,' she said, and I thought I saw a little moisture in her eyes as she spoke, 'but the fact is that for a month or two I shall be rather engaged. There is no reason why I should not tell you that we are to leave our rooms opposite and that I am to be married next Wednesday. When we have settled down, I shall be only too happy to carry out your kind commission.'

'Allow me to wish you every happiness in the great step which you are taking,' said I, opening the door and bowing, for she had risen to go. 'You will let me know where to find you. You must not be allowed to forget the fine arts altogether among your household cares.'

'No fear of that,' she said, with a bright smile. 'He is as fond of them as I am. Goodbye, sir – and many thanks for your encouragement.' Her gloved hand came out hesitatingly as though she were not sure whether she were taking a liberty or not, but I solved the question by capturing it and giving it a friendly little shake. Fare-thee-well, my earnest little wholesome woman, may the Fates be good to thee, and thy road through life be as bright and pleasant as thyself!

So she is going off to fulfil the great female destiny – to become the supplement of a man.[129] I am conscious of a vague feeling of discontent when I think of it, and yet what higher mission can she perform? It will be best for her, and assuredly best for him. The highest of men and the noblest of women are incomplete, mutilated fragmentary creatures, as long as they are single. Do what they may to persuade themselves that their unnatural state is the happiest, they are still full of vague unrests, of dim ill-defined dissatisfaction, of a tendency to narrow ways and petty thoughts. Alone, each is a half-made creature with every instinct and feeling yearning for its missing moiety.[130] Together, the man and the woman form a complete and symmetrical whole, the mind of each strongest where that of the other most needs reinforcing. Whatever may happen in this world, I am convinced that in the next, every male soul will have a female one attached to it, or combined with it, to round it off and give it symmetry. So thought the old Mormon who adduced it as an argument in favour of his creed. 'You cannot,' said he, 'take your money, your railway, or your mining stocks into the next world with you; but our marriage is not only for life but for eternity, and we shall have our wives and children with us, and so make a good start in the world to come.'[131]

These sentiments may sound a little out of place when coming from a grizzly-haired old fellow who has let half a century go by him without entering into the holy state, but then I have never been a bachelor by conviction. When the Cherub who conducts the matrimonial department in Heaven was arranging the matches of the future, he overlooked me, or muddled me up with someone of the same name, and that's why I have no one sitting in the armchair over there. Perhaps it may have been my own fault too. You see, a very large part of my life has been spent in out of the way parts of the world where, though there were plenty of people of the other sex, there were no women – womanhood being, to my mind, a mental rather than a physical distinction. Then again, I was a very shy young fellow before I started off upon my wanderings, though like the hero of Goldsmith's play I could be forward enough where shyness would have been a virtue.[132] But a well-bred woman with her wonderful inexplicable garments, her quiet self-possession, and the calm critical eyes with which she surveyed every wriggle of the large-jointed youth before her, was always in those days a very awesome spectacle to me. How often I have wished, like Emerson's shy friend, that I could slip off my corporeal jacket and steal away into the back stars there to enjoy a little assured solitude.[133] And along with this unreasonable fear went an equally unreasonable dislike towards every man who appeared to be more at his ease with them than I did myself. Well, thank Heaven, I think I have realised by this time that there are too many real miseries in the world for us to make ourselves unhappy over imaginary and artificial ones. In my case, shyness led to Bohemianism, and Bohemianism to a wandering life, and a wandering life to Bachelordom, and hence to the fact that I am alone in my second-floor front, pouring out my own colchicum and rubbing in my own liniments.

Mrs Rundle knows all about the coming marriage. Women seem to have a sixth sense which sends a warning thrill through them if there is anything matrimonial in the wind. 'Which the young man,' she explained, 'was a master at Dr Oliver's old school, and was mad in love with her for years but didn't like to speak, having no prospects, and she being reckoned an heiress. When the school broke down, though, and her father lost everything, it happened that this master came into money unexpectedly, and with this he has started another school in a different part of the country, and now he has come and told her how long he has loved her and that all is ready for her father as well as herself if she will but be his wife. Which he acted like a gentleman,' continued

Mrs Rundle energetically, 'and did a good day's work for himself as well, though it's not a good time for a young couple to start keeping house, with prime cuts at never less than eleven pence and no butter fit to put on the table under one and two pence a pound. But the queerest thing is that it turns out that she has always in her own heart been very partial to this master, but of course was that proud that she would never let him see it, so now it has all come out beautiful, which it never would have done if her father hadn't come to ruin. Which is an example of what good Mr Josiah Branter said from the pulpit the last Sunday that ever was, when he told us that we should be thankful for our troubles, for they were only sent by Providence to make the road clear for the blessings that are to come.' So for Mrs Rundle, and a great deal more, for she is a garrulous soul and her thoughts are all so tangled that when she tries to produce one, a dozen or more are sure to come trailing out at the tail of it.

I have been reading part of Tourguenieff's *Fathers and Sons* this morning – for about the fifth time, I think – and finding it as attractive as ever.[134] What is there about the book which casts a glamour over me and many others who have read it? It cannot be the subject exactly, because that hinges upon Russian political life and other matters of which we have small knowledge. Neither is it the plot, for there is hardly any, nor the humour for the same reason. Perhaps it is that the characters all give one the impression of being thoroughly in earnest about something, and earnestness is always an attraction in this lackadaisical age. Certainly a Russian novelist has splendid material to work with. The dreamy Slavonic nature with its placid surface and its fierce undercurrent of savagery and passion is a better basis of romance than can be furnished by any breed of the old steady-going Teutonic stock. Men of the type of Suwarrow and Romanzow in history or of Bazarof in fiction can only be grown on a soil where a very thin top-dressing of civilisation overlies the barbarism of ages – and their effectiveness as character studies is shown up by the background of nihilism, autocracy and Siberianism against which they live and move.[135] Such a condition of things, coupled with the ferment which has been going on for years back in the Russian mind, is sure to produce a striking national literature of which Tourguenieff is the latest, but probably by no means the final or the highest outcome.

In what order will the nations of the world stand five hundred years hence? The question furnishes a wide field for the speculative thinker and weigher of chances. In this progressive age, when there is a stirring of dry bones in every part of the globe, the changes which may be looked for in the future are far greater and more sweeping than those which have taken place in the past. And yet, look at a map of the world of five hundred years ago, and mark the alterations which have occurred. Balance 1380 against 1880. France and England were then as now independent and powerful states. America was as yet unheard of. Spain was beginning to comb out her Moorish vermin, before entering upon that course of Empire which appears now to have vanished forever, and to have left her weaker than before she embarked upon it. In Germany poor Wenzel, 'a thin violent creature,' according to Carlyle, 'over-fond of white Prague beer and of pretty girls of all complexions,'[136] was ruling the Holy Roman Empire composed of all manner of turbulent and semi-independent states. One of the smallest and most insignificant of these was that Kurfurstship of Brandenburg which has in our own day, under the name of Prussia, reunited the greater part of the German-speaking states in a more homogeneous and more powerful Empire. Italy, which has now developed into a stately nation, worthy of her grand traditions, was then a congeries of petty principalities – some prosperous and some the reverse – but one and all absorbed in their own parochial concerns. In Russia, the Dukes of Moscow exercised some sort of precarious sovereignty over barbarous Muscovite chieftains and their skinclad retainers. In Greece and along the Eastern shores of the Mediterranean, successive invasions of warlike and fanatical Musselmans were arousing the attention of Europe to the great Ottoman power, which after consolidating itself in Asia Minor was destined to take Constantinople and to found the great and aggressive state which has now sunk into such a condition of weakness and corruption. No English foot – unless it be that of the profound and accomplished liar, Sir John Maundeville,[137] had ever yet set foot upon India, and that unhappy country, just recovering from the effects of the invasion of Genghis Khan, was on the eve of the far more terrible and disastrous expedition of Timur the Tartar. The great Empire of China, sunk in a profound lethargy, was then what it has been to within the memory of our fathers, an ancient self-contained state desiring nothing and fearing nothing from the rest of the world, and absorbed in the contemplation of its own proportions and past grandeur. Switzerland had already entered upon her sturdy career of independence, and Poland was a flourishing country, but Holland had not yet shown any signs of her future greatness, and the continent of Africa, save its Mediterranean coast-line, was wrapped in impenetrable gloom. In the whole world, then, England, France, Switzerland and China appear to be the only nations which preserve more or less the same boundaries and the same relative power and position which they did five hundred years ago.

And how about the next five hundred? In what direction is expansion most likely to occur? There are four existing powers which promise to assume enormous proportions in the future, but in each case there is an ominous 'if' which may mar their development. The first, and to my mind the most certain, of these dominant empires of the 24th century is that of China. With her 300,000,000 of patient industrious inhabitants, persevering, frugal, and quick to learn, bound together by an intense patriotism and sustained by the recollection of her great history extending back like a streak of light through the twilight of the human race, she is bound to regain her proper position at the head of the nations of the earth. Already there are signs that the great sleeper is tossing uneasily, preparatory to a waking which will startle the world. Since her energetic little northern neighbour is up and doing, she cannot afford to tarry longer. Railways, education, ironclads, improved methods of agriculture and of commerce, machinery, breechloaders – they are one and all assisting the Celestials in opening out and in defending their great resources. The day is at hand when China will go in heart and soul for Western civilisation – and from that day she will be a steadily increasing and most important factor in the world's affairs.

The United States must take the second place, I think, in a speculation as to the comparative power of the countries of the future. If she can preserve her unity amid the fierce conflicts between capital and labour, and the stormy phases of Socialism, she should by that time rival China in population and exceed her in wealth and resources. As she increases in population, however, and as her soil becomes more thickly occupied, there will be a sharper contrast and a keener antagonism between the poor and the rich, which may conceivably lead to a war of classes. After emerging scatheless, however, from such a war as that of 1862, it is not probable that our great offspring will ever come to hurt. That she may thrive and prosper should be the heartfelt wish of every Englishman who has bowels for his own kindred.[138]

Our own British Empire should certainly be included among the first three of the claimants for greatness in the future. We cover a larger and more populous area of the globe than any of our rivals, but we lack homogeneousness. Strong and tough as our heart is, the giant limbs of our empire are not firmly connected with each other or with the central trunk. If statesmen can overcome this defect, and can knit all our scattered dependencies into one complete unit, then our prospects are the highest and most glorious of any. Come what may with our insular position, our mineral advantages, and our 35,000,000 of home population, we shall always play a high part in the world's history.

Russia may take the fourth place in the coming order of things. She has 80,000,000 souls under her flag and there is plenty of room for expansion in the vast central Asian steppes. It is possible, however, that when the grand crash comes, and the present despotism goes down before the irresistible demand for reform, the convulsion may have the effect of rending the empire apart. The trans-Ural provinces, for example, being less advanced and less well informed than the European, might possibly refuse to acquiesce in the new order of things, and might proclaim their independence and elect some exiled Romanoff or some ambitious general as their ruler. There are so many possibilities in the future for every state that it would be rash indeed to make too confident a prediction. One can hardly, however, be wrong in setting down China, the States, Britain and Russia as the four countries which have the widest prospects before them. Germany, especially when she has absorbed the German-speaking provinces of Austria, and France will always remain great and independent nations, but it is geographically impossible for them to attain to the colossal dimensions to which the others may aspire.

Now I think I foreswore prophecy at the very beginning of my notes, and here I am at it again as bad as ever. It shows a want of judgement when a man begins to lay down the law as to what is going to happen this year or the next, for the chances are that his pretensions to foresight are snuffed out by some sudden and unlooked-for turn of events. Lord Jeffrey remarking that Byron's poems 'would not do,'[139] Wordsworth asserting that Shelley's name would not live, or the anonymous critic counselling Anthony Trollope to give up writing novels, for which he had no natural bent, are all examples of gentlemen who have made forecasts as to the future which have not added to their reputation for acumen. Now if they had only adopted my method, and projected their speculations out for a few hundred years, they might have gained some little credit, and certainly avoided any chance of ever knowing that the facts had been ill-advised enough to arrange differently to their speculation. There is nothing absolutely certain except the uncertainty of all things, and nothing that we thoroughly know except our own complete want of knowledge. I have a great regard and esteem for science, but of all the contemptible and exasperating insects who crawl upon this sphere, I think the unimaginative complacent type of scientist is the most unbearable – the man who knows very exactly all that he does know, but has not sense enough to understand what a speck his little accumulation of doubtful erudition is when compared with the immensity of our ignorance. 'There is no mystery in the matter,' says this prodigy, with his eyebrows in the air. 'The world is ruled by certain definite laws, and what applies to us applies equally no doubt to every other heavenly body. There is gravity which determines our relation to the firmament in general, and there is evolution which explains why we are as we are, and there are the laws of geology to explain to us what manner of earth we are inhabiting. It is all settled by laws which have been investigated and laid down by science.' That is the way in which our sapient friend settles the matter offhand, and yet he will howl about bigotry and narrow-mindedness. What could be more bigoted and paltry than this scientific shibboleth of his, this wretched word-juggling, this polysyllabic hypocrisy which fills a man with wind when he has most need of solid nourishment? It has been said that the fanaticism of some of the early reformers is to be excused because, if they had not been zealots, they would have had no chance of holding their own against the enthusiasts who were opposed to them. Perhaps something of the same sort may be said for the more hidebound of our scientists, and their attitude of absolute negation may be a set-off against those gentlemen who believe that the world was created on the 23rd of October of the year 4004 BC – if any such remain. *In medio tutissimus ibis.*[140]

The world is governed *according to* laws, but that is a very different thing from being governed *by* laws. The more we pry into the methods by which results are brought about, the more stupendous and wonderful becomes the great unseen power which lies behind them. Now, what is that power? What is the intelligence which has planned out this marvellous piece of work? Now, my scientific friend, here is a 300-diameter Hartknack's microscope,[141] and here is a telescope with a six-foot speculum. You may pry and peep through one or other for the remainder of your natural existence, and if you can tell us at the end of it a word about the motive power which has set the universe going, you shall have a mausoleum which shall out-do that of King Cheops. You are in the position of a man who is forever examining and praising a great picture, and who, having satisfied himself that the account given him of the painting of the picture is incorrect, at once concludes that no one ever painted it, or at least asserts that he has no possible means of knowing whether an artist had produced it or not. 'Is not the existence of the picture a proof that an artist – and a very skilful artist – has been engaged upon it?' one might ask. 'Why, no,' says the learned man. 'It is possible that the picture produced itself by the aid of certain rules. Besides, when this picture was first shown to me, I was assured that it had been all produced within a week, but by examining it I am able to say with certainty that it has taken a very long time to put together. I am therefore of the opinion that it is doubtful whether anyone ever painted it at all.' 'But we see that it is painted, and there must therefore have been a painter,' cries the bewildered enquirer. 'I cannot allow that,' answers the wise one. 'I really cannot give you an opinion on the matter. I am a know-not, an agnostic.' That is the high-water mark which human wisdom has reached – to date.

Now this, as in the case of Knox and his crew, is simply a reaction against the intolerable pedantry of the Christian churches, with their hysterical doctrines and their insufferable pretensions to special bolstering-up from Providence.[142] When a man realises that he does not know everything, he is too apt to fly to the conclusion that he knows nothing. There is a strange distorted satisfaction in the exaggeration of his own ignorance, just as a sufferer from some deforming complaint comes occasionally to take a pride in his own malady, and to exhibit it with complacency. But if you probe into this profession of agnosticism, you will find that it is quite as far from the truth, and has even less to commend it than the dogmatism of the churchmen. All the philosophic definitions and chemical formulae that have ever been evolved cannot get over the fact that the world exists, and that whatever exists must have had a conceiver and originator. Call that first cause, or what you will, but recognise in it infinite power and infinite solicitude for the wants of all created beings. We need no inspired volume, nor anything but our own eyes and brains to come to that conclusion, but having reached it, what becomes of agnosticism? Why say you know nothing when you *do* know something – and that something the very basis and core of religion? One would think that the reasoning was plain enough, but you cannot corner your pseudo-scientist in that way. He is off, like a cuttlefish, in a cloud of ink, and you are lucky if he leaves behind him an admission that there may exist an 'unanthropomorphic transparency' or some other madness of the kind. *Il n'y a point de sots si incommodes que ceux qui ont de l'esprit.*[143]

By the way, I remember a few days ago, when I was moralising in one of my minor keys about the origin of evil, I endeavoured to set forth that the hurricane, the lightning, pain, disease, and many other things which appear to us to detract from the benevolence of the Creator are really – could we but see into them – among his choicest gifts. I have noticed since, on looking over my Paley,[144] that he throws a light upon one at least of these phenomena. If you put foul air into a bottle with a little water, says he, and shake them up together, you will remove all the impurity. When a tempest lashes the sea into foam, the very same process is being carried on on an enormous scale. Were it not for these periodical cleansings, the whole atmosphere would soon become so loaded with carbon and impurities of all sorts that it would be poisonous to our lungs. It may be true or it may not, but it shows at any rate how hard it is to distinguish a blessing from a curse. There is nothing which may not prove eventually to have been of benefit to us – except perhaps rheumatic gout.

All these theological disquisitions are prompted by the fact that about three o'clock this afternoon I had a visit from no less an individual than the senior curate of the parish – a long thin gentleman with a sad pale face and a subdued manner. I have no love for the cloth. A long experience has convinced me that just as cotton, which is a harmless substance enough in itself, becomes dangerous on being dipped into nitric acid, so the mildest of mortals is to be feared when once he has inoculated himself with sectarian religion. If he has any capacity for rancour or hardness in him, it will bring it out. I was therefore by no means overjoyed to see my visitor, though I received him with due courtesy and begged him to be seated.

Mrs Rundle attended at his church, he explained, and he had heard that one of her lodgers was ill. He had considered it to be his duty to call and see if he could be of any service to me. Was very glad to perceive that I was regaining my health and hoped I would soon be able to get about again. He spoke in rather a high and yet husky voice, and had a way of dropping it at the last few words of each sentence which jarred rather upon my ear. His long white quivering fingers too, which played nervously with the little cross which hung from his watch chain, annoyed and fidgeted me. I thanked him, however, for his kindness in calling upon me with all the cordiality which I could command.[145]

'You see, the Vicar has been away in the South of France for his health,' he explained, 'and we have to do the best we can to look after things in his absence. He has been away for nearly two years.'

'The parish must miss him very much,' I remarked politely.

'Well, he never lived in the parish,' said the Curate. 'You see, he is a man who has always been accustomed to live in very good style, and there was no house in the parish large enough for his requirements. He is a very distinguished man of good family, and we may consider ourselves fortunate in having his services.'

I was too much bewildered at this view of the matter to make any reply. Before I could quite recover from my wonder, the Curate, who had been eyeing me closely, remarked, 'You must have been only a short time among us. I cannot recollect having ever seen your face in Church.'

'No,' said I. 'I never go to church.'

'Not a dissenter,' cried my visitor, half rising from his chair with disgust expressed upon every feature of his face. 'I did not understand from Mrs Rundle that you were a dissenter.'

'Neither I am.'

'Oh, quite so – I see,' he said playfully, with a look of relief. 'A little lax – a little negligent. Well, well, men of the world get into these ways. They have much to distract their attentions. You at least cling fast to the fundamental truths of Christianity – you believe those in your heart.'

'I believe from the bottom of my heart,' said I, 'that Jesus Christ was the sweetest and best character of whom we have any record in the history of this planet.'

'I trust that your belief goes deeper than that,' said the Curate severely. 'You are surely prepared to admit that he was an incarnation of the Godhead.'

'But it appears to me,' I objected, 'that if he were but a frail mortal like ourselves, his life assumes a deep significance as showing how pure and how lofty a human existence may be. It becomes a standard towards which we may work. If, on the other hand, he was intrinsically of a different nature to ourselves, then his existence loses its point since we and he start on a different basis. To my mind, such a supposition takes away all the beauty and all the moral of his life. If he was divine, then he could not sin, and there was an end of the matter. We who are not divine, and who can sin, have little to learn from a life like that. It is a cheap triumph. You remember the Emperor Commodus, who used to descend into the arena fully armed and pit himself against some poor wretch who had only a leaden sword given him which would double up if he used it? According to your theory of Christ's life, you would have it that he faced the temptations of the world at such an advantage that they were but harmless leaden things, and not the sharp terrible assailants which we find them. I prefer to look upon Christ as a sweet, loving elder brother, who came down as we have come down into this arena of life, and who, without any sheltering halo of divinity, fought a fair fight against the very enemies which we have to face, and showed how easy it was to conquer them.'

'Why, you are nothing else than a Unitarian, sir,' cried the Curate with a pink flush upon his white cheeks.

'You may label me as you like,' said I. 'I have been looking for truth this thirty years, and though I may not have got much further, I at least have come to some pretty certain conclusions as to what is *not* truth. It is not true that religion reached its acme nineteen hundred years ago, and that we are forever to refer back to what was written and said in those times. No, sir. Religion is a vital living thing, still growing and working, and

capable of endless extension and development like all other fields
of thought. There were some eternal truths spoken of old, and
handed down to us in a book which may truly be called holy. But
there are other eternal truths yet to be revealed, and if we are to
reject them because they are not to be found in those pages, you
will do as wisely as a scientist who would have nothing to say to
Kirshhoff's spectral analysis because there is no mention of it in
Albertus Magnus. There are prophets now as there were prophets
then. Our modern prophet wears a broadcloth coat and writes
for *The Nineteenth Century*, but he may none the less be the little
pipe which conveys a tiny rill from the inexhaustible reservoirs
of eternal truth.[146] I have a text there, sir, over the door – "One
way or another all the light, energy, and available virtue which
we have does come out of us, and goes very infallibly into God's
treasury living and working through eternities there. We are not
lost – not a single atom of us – of one of us."[147] Now that has the
ring of religious truth about it, and yet came from no Hebrew
lips, but from a very worthy man down Chelsea way. I don't know
that God Almighty has declared that he has said his last say to
the Human Race. It is as easy for him to speak through Carlyle
the Scotchman as through Jeremiah the Jew. The Bible, sir, is a
book which comes out in instalments, and "To be continued,"
not "finis," is written at the end of it. We may expect a further
supplement one of these days.'

My visitor had been showing every sign of acute uneasiness
during this long speech of mine, but as he listened to my conclud-
ing words he sprang to his feet and seized his soft black hat in a
paroxysm of indignation.

'Your opinions are highly dangerous, sir,' said he. 'I never
listened to sadder infidelity. You believe in nothing.'

'I believe in nothing which limits the power or the goodness
or the justice of God,' I answered.

'You have evolved all this from your own spiritual pride and
self sufficiency,' said he hotly. 'Why do you not pray to that Deity
whose name you use? Why do you not humble yourself before
Him and ask for a little saving faith?'

'How do you know I don't?' I asked.

'You said yourself that you never went to church.'

'I carry my own church about under my own hat,' said I. 'Bricks and mortar won't make a ladder into heaven. I believe with Christ that the human heart is the best temple. I am sorry to see that you differ from him on this point.'

Perhaps it was too bad of me to say that. I might have guarded myself without countering. Anyhow, it had the effect of ending an interview which was becoming somewhat oppressive. My visitor was too indignant to answer, and bounced out of the room and down the stairs without another word. From my window I can see him streaming down the street, a poor little black angry thing, very hot and troubled because he can't measure the whole universe with his pocket square and compass. Think of it, and think of what he is, an atom among atoms, standing at the meeting point of two eternities. But what am I, a brother-atom, that I should judge him!

After all, might it not have been better had I listened to what he had to say without obtruding my own views? If he is happy in his beliefs, I should be sorry indeed to controvert them. Yet we can but say what we believe to be truth after having sought it out in the silence of our own hearts. Is it not a duty to speak out against the narrower and less comprehensive views, for the true creed *must* be as broad as the Universe itself, and therefore infinitely broader than anything which the mind of man can conceive? A protest against sectarian ways of thought must always be an aspiration towards truth. The great Creator is no God of cliques, but has all this vast universe in his keeping. Who shall dare to claim a monopoly of him, or to limit his loving kindness? Surely it is there that the real impiety lies.

I had hoped that the Major would have come in today, but I have seen no sign of him, though his crisp military step may be heard on the floor above. I fear that he has met with ill success at the War Office.[148] Down below, Herr Lehmann bangs and crashes on the grand piano. Perhaps in some future avatar the Herr Professor may be transformed into one of those *pneumora* whose whole bodies serve as musical instruments. By the way, is it not a fact that we exalt our auditory apparatus unduly at the expense of some of our other faculties? Our olfactory nerves, for example, are as sensitive and as delicate as our sense of hearing, yet we do not hear of their producing the refined and spiritual and ethereal effects which are said to arise from the higher developments of music. There is no reason why a brain-stimulation through smell should be less suggestive than a brain-stimulation through sound. Why should not some olfactory Mendelssohn of the future arrange a series of scents without words, which should convey as dreamy and poetical an effect as their musical prototypes? Why should we not have studies in frangi panni or a symphony in Attar of Roses with a musk accompaniment? Who knows that there may not be a scent opera in the days to come, which shall blend all manner of expressive and artistically arranged perfumes, from the violets which mark the entrance of the rustic heroine to the whiff of asafoetida or brimstone which heralds the approach of the villain. Indeed, when one thinks of it, there is an infinitely greater variety in scent than in sound, and a composer may launch forth upon that field without any fear of plagiarising from the works of his predecessors. Mr Gilbert could not do better than discard Mr Sullivan and take Mr Rimmel into a literary and odoriferous partnership.[149]

I confess that I am somewhat of a Philistine in this matter of music, nor am I at all convinced that the musical ear is in itself a mark of refinement. Some of the most delicate-minded sensitive highly-strung men whom I have known have confessed to me that they were in the position of the historical personage who could only recognise two tunes, one of which was 'God save the Queen' and the other wasn't. On the other hand, I very well remember that at Singapore in the old days the Malays and lascars could pick up any tune after hearing it once, and reproduce it on their violins. Their musical sense amounted almost to an instinct, and yet I don't think their best friends would claim refinement as one of their virtues. In its higher developments the musical faculty may be elevating and aesthetic, but you won't find among your own friends that there is any direct ratio between their mental or even their emotional capacity and their ear for music. Darwin states somewhere that men probably conversed by means of musical sounds before they had learned to frame words, which would make our composers and performers mere reversions to a lower type. There is a German band playing at the other end of the street which would lend itself to the theory.

What a heavy, heavy day! Nothing but grumbling and disputing, and treading on my neighbours' corns! Let me wind up with a few verses on a subject which we can all agree upon. The Major was narrating the other day the devotion of some of our rank and file in Egypt, and lamenting that poor Tommy Atkins[150] and his individual doings seldom found their way into the dispatches. As Lowell sang,

> 'Somehow when we've fought and licked, I always found
>   the thanks
> Got kind of lodged before they reached as low down as
>   the ranks'[151]

The thought has been running in my mind, together with a particular example of gallantry – one of many which had come under his notice – with the result that it suddenly crystallised out into a string of verses which I have named:

Corporal Dick's Promotion[152]

The Eastern day was well high o'er
When, parched with thirst and travel-sore
Two of McPherson's Army Corps
Across the desert were tramping.
They had wandered off from the beaten track
And now were wearily harking back,
Ever glancing round for the Union Jack
Which marked their comrades camping.

The first was Lance-Corporal Robert Dick,
Bearded and burly, short and thick,
Rough of speech and in temper quick,

A sullen old dog and a surly.
The other, fresh from his mother's care,
Was a young recruit, smooth-cheeked and fair,
With a face as fresh as the English air
And his flaxen hair all curly.

Jaded and spent and hunger-torn
They had wandered on from early morn
And the young recruit was all forlorn
Silent – his troubles nursing.
Save a desert jackal dining alone,
And snarling over a half-gnawed bone
Not a sound broke in on the monotone
Of the Corporal's muttered cursing.

But far to westward a rolling cloud,
The sandy spray from a moving crowd,
Darkens the air, like a sombre shroud
Against the background of azure.
Rifts in the whirling wreaths reveal
Shadowy riders and glint of steel
While the tawny clouds all else conceal
Like the smoke from a fort's embrasure.

The Corporal glanced at the darkening west,
Stuck his pipe in his khaki vest,
Growled out an oath and onward pressed
Still glancing over his shoulder.
'Bedouins, mate!' he curtly said
'We'll have some work for steel and lead
'And, maybe, sleep on a sandy bed
'Before we're one hour older!'

Side by side with pain and toil,
Ankle-deep in the yielding soil
They staggered along – while a wild turmoil
Rose from the distant foeman.

Swiftly the Arab warriors sped
But far in front their Chieftain led,
Riding a charger desert-bred
With a vulture flapping over his head
A dark portentous omen.

Nearer yet and yet more near
Thundering on in his wild career
He brandished high his gleaming spear
With a smile on his swarthy features.
At the sound of his hoofs the pair faced round,
Dogged and grim they stood their ground,
With never a word save a sharp fierce sound,
Like the snarl of hunted creatures.

Says Corporal Dick with a rugged frown,
'First come, first served! We must fetch him down!
'Aim steady and true or I lay you a crown
'That we've reached the end of the chapter!'
A sputter of fire – a cry of pain –
The blue smoke drifting over the plain –
The Chief is down and his charger's rein
Is in the hands of its captor.

With the light of hope upon his face
The Corporal sprang in the dead man's place,
He knew the gallant stallion's pace,
Rejoicing to bestride him.
But ere upon his course he flew
One hurried glance around he threw,
And he met the wistful eyes so blue
Of the young recruit beside him.

'Twas but a flash – a fleeting dart,
But it pierced the rough old soldier's heart,
He sprang to earth. 'Up, up and start!
'They'll be on us in less than a minute!

'Up with you! No palaver! Go!
'I'll bide behind and run the show
'Promotion has been cursed slow
'And this is my chance to win it.'

Into the saddle he thrust him quick,
Spurred up the steed with a bayonet prick,
Watched it gallop with plunge and with kick
Away o'er the desert careering.
Then he turned with a softened face,
Loosening the strap of his cartridge case,
While his thoughts flew back to the dear old place,
In the sunny Hampshire clearing.

His young companion gazing back
Saw the pursuers' wild attack
And heard the sharp Martini crack
But as he looked already
The dark fanatic Arab band
Were closing in on every hand
Until a whirling wreath of sand
Concealed them in its eddy.

A squadron of British horse that night
Galloping hard through the shadowy light
Came on the scene of that last stern fight
And found the Corporal lying
Silent and grim on the trampled sand,
With his rifle grasped in his stiffened hand,
Like a sentry waiting his last command
Mid a ring of the dead and dying.[153]

And still when twilight shadows fall
After the evening bugle call
In bivouac and in barrack hall
They tell the tale of the Corporal
His death and his devotion.

And when they speak of him they say
That perhaps a hidden meaning lay
In the words he spoke, and that the day
When his rough bold spirit passed away
Was the day that he won promotion.

CHAPTER 6

WORK A MAN can bear with, but rest is very exhausting. Here have I been lying idle for six long days, and I am as heartily weary as a man can be. But the Doctor is very consoling. Tomorrow if I continue to improve I am to have an hour and a half in the open air. I can walk quite comfortably up and down the room.

'Why don't you find the bacterium of rheumatism, Doctor,' said I. 'If you could manage to sterilise that, we would build a monument to you as high as the Eiffel Tower.'

'Who knows?' said he, laughing. 'Who knows? It has been considered to arise from chemical change, but one of these little invisible miscreants may prove to be at the bottom of it.'

'How preposterous it seems,' I remarked. 'We are like some defenceless country with open frontiers, exposed to the invasion of every wild tribe of microbes who choose to attack us.'

'Very true. But you have an admirably drilled standing army for your defence.'

'In my case, then,' said I, 'the standing army appears to have been defeated, and I am falling back upon my auxiliary forces.'

'Not at all. It has been a contest of six days, but your guards have been victorious. You have read, I presume, the recent investigations on the subject of the functions of the leucocytes.'

'No, I have not seen them.'

'They outdo the wildest dreams of Romance. You know what a leucocyte is? They are little microscopic jelly-like creatures which are found drifting along in our bloodstream.'

'White blood corpuscles?'

'Exactly so. There are millions of them in the human body,

but their function has never been made out, and the general view among physiologists was that they were purposeless little blobs of jelly, or at least that they performed some very minor office in the system. It has now, however, been very clearly made out by recent experiment that these creatures are the most trusty and energetic friends of the human race – the special bodyguards and household troops which garrison his system.'

'And how that?' I asked.

And here the manuscript ends, mid-page.

NOTE ON THE MANUSCRIPT

THIS TEXT has been published from an untitled manuscript that was among the Conan Doyle papers sold at auction in 2004 and acquired by the British Library. This manuscript, we may safely assume, constitutes the novel as Conan Doyle reconstructed it from memory after it had been lost in the post on its way to the publishers.

The manuscript is written in four A4 sized notebooks which are hardcover and bound in black cloth. Filled with neat and easily readable handwriting, the 154 pages they contain have been numbered by Conan Doyle. The manuscript appears to be part fair copy and part working document. The first half of the first notebook shows evidence of reasonably thorough re-working: there are a number of words – in some cases a number of lines – crossed out and re-written on almost every page; at a couple of points some marginal revisions have also been added. There are also several pages in the first notebook where parts of a page (often half or more) have been cut away. By contrast, the text in the latter half of the first notebook and in the remaining notebooks shows only the odd word or couple of words crossed out and corrected. Many of the pages are completely clear.

The evidence of the physical manuscript, then, clearly demonstrates that this is a rewriting and that Conan Doyle at some point was engaged in revising his text, doing a more thorough job on the early stages before other projects took his attention elsewhere. The unfinished nature of the text (Chapter 6 in the fourth notebook comprises only two pages, written in a different ink from the rest of the manuscript) also underlines that this was a work-in-progress for Conan Doyle.

NOTES

Introduction

1. An expression commonly applied in Scotland and the north of England to enterprises begun in youthful ardour without experience. Sir Walter Scott, one of Conan Doyle's earliest literary enthusiasms, had used it in *Rob Roy*.
2. *Arthur Conan Doyle: A Life in Letters*, ed. Jon Lellenberg, Daniel Stashower and Charles Foley (New York: Penguin Press; London: HarperPress, 2007), p. 167.
3. Sir Arthur Conan Doyle, *Memories and Adventures* (London: Hodder & Stoughton, 1924), p. 17.
4. *Arthur Conan Doyle: A Life in Letters*, p. 173.
5. Ibid., p. 229.
6. Ibid., p. 207.
7. Ibid., p. 229.
8. 'I have written 130 pages of the novel, but have laid it aside pro tem in favour of a short story which may do for Cornhill. I wrote 8 pages of it yesterday and so far it is very good.' *Arthur Conan Doyle: A Life in Letters*, p. 202.
9. Ibid., p. 224.
10. His eldest son, Kingsley, was studying medicine there at the time.

The Narrative of John Smith

1. Gout, a far more common complaint those days, was something Conan Doyle encountered in his medical studies, and kept up with, publishing a letter about 'The Remote Effects of Gout' in the *Lancet* for 29 November 1884. In 1899 he made another protagonist someone laid up by gout, in the story 'A Question of Diplomacy' in his medical stories collection *Round the Red Lamp*. 'We [novelists] do not fly to extremes in our literary ailments,' he joked before a London audience of medical men in 1905: 'The only example which I know to the contrary is gout, which in all our pages only occurs in the ball of the big toe. For some reason it is usually treated as a semi-comic disease, which tends to prove that the novelist has not himself suffered from it. The gouty, irascible gourmand is one of our necessary puppets, and I am sure he has every reason to be irascible if contempt is invited for his very serious and painful malady.'
2. For Conan Doyle, a snuff-box appears to have been an insignia of the Victorian physician as much as the stethoscope became. 'Time was, my dear colleague,' says a physician in his 1926 novel *The Land of Mist*, 'when a snuff-box was as much a part of my equipment as my phlebotomy case.'
3. Colchicum and alkalis are both mentioned as treatments for gout in Conan

Doyle's 1884 *Lancet* article. The first may have been of particular interest to him, because colchicum had been used by mid-nineteenth-century British poisoner Catherine Wilson, a nurse who murdered patients after being written into their wills, and was hanged for one of these murders in 1862. 'When a doctor goes wrong he is the first of criminals,' declared Sherlock Holmes in the story 'The Speckled Band,' and Conan Doyle was aware that nurses also had criminally useful knowledge, as doctors did.

4. An opiate, therefore addictive.

5. Not all Conan Doyle's characters would have been averse to such languid periods: Sherlock Holmes could spend days at a time lying on the sofa at Baker Street.

6. A statement Conan Doyle could make about himself until very late in his life.

7. John Milton. Conan Doyle used his observation again in his 1889 psychic novel *The Mystery of Cloomber.*

8. Thomas Gray, *Elegy Written in a Country Churchyard.*

9. 'We lived in the hardy and bracing atmosphere of poverty,' Conan Doyle wrote of himself and his siblings in his 1924 autobiography *Memories and Adventures,* 'and we each in turn did our best to help those who were younger than ourselves.' The following four hundred words express a key element of Conan Doyle's lifelong philosophy, though it was a genteel poverty in which he was raised in Edinburgh. Nor did many children of poverty get to attend England's leading Jesuit boarding school Stonyhurst College as he did, starting in 1867. See *Arthur Conan Doyle: A Life in Letters,* ch. 1.

10. Thomas Babington Macaulay, the poet, historian and politician. 'When I visited London at the age of sixteen the first thing I did after housing my luggage was to make a pilgrimage to Macaulay's grave where he lies in Westminster Abbey,' Conan Doyle wrote in *Through the Magic Door.*

11. Presumably Henry Wriothesley, third Earl of Southampton (1573–1624), and a patron of Shakespeare, whose sole surviving son Henry, the fourth Earl (1607–1667), had only daughters.

12. Conan Doyle never had a bustling practice of his own, but had worked several times during medical school and immediately afterwards for Dr Reginald Ratcliffe Hoare of Birmingham, who became a second father to Conan Doyle for years. His practice was such a one: 'a five-horse city practice,' Conan Doyle said of it, which 'meant going from morning to night.'

13. Thomas Carlyle, the Scottish historian and critic (1795–1881), was one of Conan Doyle's favourite and most frequently quoted writers. Carlyle handed over most of his private papers before his death to the historian and biographer James Anthony Froude (1818–1894). A close friend, later his executor, Froude had undertaken editions of Jane Carlyle's letters and Carlyle's reminiscences as well as a full-scale biography (the *Life of Carlyle,* published in two parts), all of which appeared in an intense concentration of activity beginning one month after Carlyle's death and ending in 1884. Froude's *Life* caused considerable controversy on account of its frankness of treatment, particularly about his subject's failings of character and unhappy marriage, which damaged Carlyle's reputation. By the time Conan Doyle was writing the *Narrative* he would have read most or all of these (he reports reading the *Life* in a letter home), and seems, in the passages here, to be directly defending his hero against Froude's claims.

14. Thomas Fuller (1608–1661), churchman, historian, author of *The Holy State and the Profane State* (1642), but misquoted here, the original being: 'Anger is one of the sinews of the soul; he that wants it hath a maimed mind.'

15. Quoting (not precisely accurately) an 1845 letter by Carlyle in Froude's *Thomas Carlyle: A History of His Life in London*. *Thatkraft*, from German historical writings, might be translated as active power, or force.

16. Thin soup or gruel.

17. The sort of thing Sherlock Holmes might have said, but here the sitting-room that John Smith describes is a close approximation of Conan Doyle's front room at Bush Villas in Southsea, down to the painted green walls and his own '17 well framed pictures 17 vases quite aesthetic,' as he referred to them in a letter home to his mother.

18. Alphonse-Marie-Adolphe de Neuville (1835–1885), whose work included Franco-Prussian War subjects, perhaps appealing to Conan Doyle who had championed the French cause in school. Noel Paton (1821–1901) was a Scottish painter in the Pre-Raphaelite style whose use of fairies and mythology may have appealed to Conan Doyle since his father and his uncle Richard Doyle were also well known for such subject matter.

19. Characters of Charles Dickens's in *Our Mutual Friend*.

20. Some of the objects he discusses next did have direct autobiographical value for him. While the Roman amphora did not represent a personal visit to Italy as yet, the Arctic memorabilia were items and experiences he acquired in six months' service as ship's surgeon aboard the Greenland whaler *Hope*, February to August 1880, during which time he said he had come of age (22 May 1880) 'at 80 degrees north latitude': 'I went on board a big, straggling youth,' he said in *Memories and Adventures*, but 'came off it a powerful, well-grown man.' Later, before coming to Southsea, he did another stint as ship's surgeon on the passenger-carrying freighter *Mayumba* to West Africa, where he had contracted a near-fatal tropical fever.

21. Inquisitive, gossipy people.

22. Hollands refers to gin by the originating country's name, probably the older 'genever' variety different from the dry gins produced in England by this time.

23. It would be welcome to know how autobiographical this incident is; it may well be. But much of our knowledge of Conan Doyle's early life comes from his frequent letters home to his mother, and while attending medical school at Edinburgh University he lived at home, and didn't write many letters to others that have come to light. He did box in these days, taking boxing gloves along on the *Hope*, and boxing with its crew members for the exercise and sport.

24. A double jab to the head.

25. Many years later, in 1907, Conan Doyle would write an entire book, *Through the Magic Door*, about his library and the books and writers it contained: 'I care not how humble your bookshelf may be, nor how lowly the room which it adorns,' he began: 'Close the door of that room behind you, shut off with it all the cares of the outer world, plunge back into the soothing company of the great dead, and then you are through the magic portal into that fair land whither worry and vexation can follow you no more.' Here, he mentions some favourites of his youth, including a few he will say more about in subsequent passages of this manuscript. They are the more elevated ones here, forgoing mention of other indisputable favourites of his early years like Edgar Allan Poe and Alexandre Dumas. William Winwood Reade (1838–1875) was a philosopher whose *The Martyrdom of Man* Sherlock Holmes once handed to Dr Watson: 'Let me recommend this book – one of the most remarkable ever penned,' discussing it further on a second occasion in the Sherlock Holmes stories. Charles Darwin, of course,

was the great naturalist whose theory of evolution Conan Doyle had embraced in medical school despite his Roman Catholic upbringing.

26. The Roman writer Horace.

27. By 1883–84 Conan Doyle had visited London several times, most notably in his mid-teens, when he stayed with his artistically distinguished London uncles. But he had not lived there so far, making this reference to Marylebone interesting: the district includes Baker Street, to be made the home of Sherlock Holmes when Conan Doyle wrote *A Study in Scarlet* in 1885. In Baker Street in 1874 the teenage Conan Doyle had visited Madame Tussaud's wax museum, whose chamber of horrors particularly pleased him: 'I have been also to Madam Tussaud's, and was delighted with the room of Horrors, and the images of the murderers,' he wrote home to his mother.

28. These lines are a fragment from a paragraph cut out of the previous page of manuscript.

29. Though humble things, gas-pipes were on his mind. For one thing, he could not initially afford gas lighting when he took Bush Villas in June 1882, and was left for some months with candles for night-time illumination. (And when he did have it laid on, its expense strained his resources.) Also: 'When the *Gas and Water Gazette* asked him to translate a German submission, Conan Doyle drew on his shaky schoolboy German to produce an article entitled "Testing Gas Pipes for Leakage." Years later, in a speech to the Authors' Club, he would claim that this had been the great breakthrough of his career, rather than *A Study in Scarlet*, as one might have supposed. For the first time, he noted dryly, a publisher had asked for his services, rather than the other way around.' (Daniel Stashower, *Teller of Tales: The Life of Arthur Conan Doyle*, Holt, New York, 2000, pp. 82–3.)

30. The London Aquarium was another sight he wrote home about as a teenager. Surprising about this reference is its flippancy regarding drunkards. His own father Charles Altamont Doyle's excessive drinking had caused the family pain and hardship, especially after his career as an artist and draughtsman terminated early, and it led to Charles Doyle's institutionalization for the remainder of life.

31. 'Tab': northern British slang for a cigarette.

32. Charles Piazzi Smyth (1819–1900), Astronomer Royal for Scotland, was the progenitor of theories about the Great Pyramid's design and construction which had a considerable vogue. Conan Doyle was always fascinated by such things, and in Southsea was already under the influence of a retired major-general named Alfred Drayson who was an amateur astronomer of some repute, author of controversial theories about the creation of the world, and the man who introduced Conan Doyle to psychic research at this time.

33. Lady Teazle and Mrs (actually also Lady) Sneerwell are characters from the 1777 play *The School for Scandal* by Richard Brinsley Sheridan (1751–1816). While Conan Doyle did not publish or even complete this rewriting of his first novel, this passage indicates that he kept the manuscript at hand for years, drawing from it occasionally for other writings of his. The preceding passage went into his semi-autobiographical novel of 1895, *The Stark Munro Letters*, and two years before that into his contribution to a non-fiction anthology entitled *My First Book*. Conan Doyle also transferred to *The Stark Munro Letters* more or less intact the earlier passage on pp. 21–2, the following one on p. 24 about dermoid cysts, plus ch. 2, pp. 34–5 and 38; ch. 3, p. 60; ch. 4, pp. 77–8; and ch. 5, pp. 87–8 and 108–12.

34. An issue which never ceased to rumble inside Conan Doyle. In his 1912 novel *The Lost World*, for example, his great scientist character Professor Challenger says to a rival: 'No, Summerlee, I will have none of your materialism, for I, at least, am too great a thing to end in mere physical constituents, a packet of salts and three bucketfuls of water.'

35. Conan Doyle speaks for himself. However far-ranging his reading and writing, he was a life-long athlete and outdoorsman, devoting a chapter of his autobiography *Memories and Adventures* to his experiences in those areas.

36. Mrs Rundle is a precursor of Mrs Hudson, Sherlock Holmes's landlady at Baker Street. Their real-life inspiration was Conan Doyle's own housekeeper at Bush Villas, a Mrs Smith, who like Mrs Rundle occupied the basement of the house, and whom he mentioned frequently in his letters home during these years.

37. 'Half-pay' refers to the reduced salary of a military officer retired or not on active service. Dr Watson refers to himself as a 'half-pay surgeon' in *The Sign of the Four*, the second Holmes tale.

38. Conan Doyle had been a boy at Stonyhurst College, a medical student at Edinburgh, and harboured hopes of becoming a literary man in London. He had travelled to the Arctic, West Africa and parts of Europe. He had not been a soldier in America, of course, though he was interested in the US Civil War, and he had not been a diamond digger at the Cape. But his first published story, 'The Mystery of Sasassa Valley,' in *Chambers' Journal* several years before, had been set in the diamond fields of South Africa.

39. A sentiment he long held, in these years of constant story submissions met usually by repeated rejection slips. 'My poor "Study" has never even been read by anyone except [the editor James] Payn,' he complained two years later to his mother, having failed so far to find a publisher for his first Sherlock Holmes tale *A Study in Scarlet*: 'Verily literature is a difficult oyster to open.'

40. As presumably the original manuscript of *The Narrative of John Smith* had been in 1883 – never to be seen again!

41. Conan Doyle had assumed the care of his young brother Innes, who had come to live with him during the summer of 1882. While he was delighted to have Innes, the responsibility for raising and educating the young boy sometimes wore heavily upon Conan Doyle during these lean years. Most of these comments about the difficulty of getting started as a writer are autobiographical in nature, and echoed in his letters in *Arthur Conan Doyle: A Life in Letters*.

42. 'Fifty little cylinders of manuscript did I send out during eight years, which described irregular orbits,' declared Conan Doyle in 1893 in *My First Book*, 'and usually came back like paper boomerangs to the place that they had started from.'

43. Conan Doyle refers to James Payn (1830–1898), once co-editor of *Chambers' Journal* and now editor of *The Cornhill*, Britain's leading literary magazine. Payn had published Conan Doyle's first story in 1879, and his true breakthrough story (though without a byline), 'J. Habakuk Jephson's Statement,' in 1883. Conan Doyle remained devoted to Payn for the older writer's life, even though, when Payn read *A Study in Scarlet* in manuscript, he had told Conan Doyle that he shouldn't waste his time with 'shilling shockers.' (In 1893 Conan Doyle came to agree, killing off the by then immensely popular Sherlock Holmes in the story 'The Final Problem.')

44. 'I determined that literature should be my staff, not my crutch, and that the profits of my literary labour, however convenient otherwise, should not, if I could help it, become necessary to my ordinary expenses.'

45. Alluding to the eighteenth-century London district known for writers at the low end of literary life. Samuel Johnson called the term 'originally the name of a street ... much inhabited by writers of small histories, dictionaries, and temporary poems, whence any mean production is called grubstreet.' In 1891 it inspired a novel by Conan Doyle's friend George Gissing entitled *New Grub Street*.

46. The Education Act of 1870 provided for compulsory universal education. In Conan Doyle's 1893 story 'The Naval Treaty,' Sherlock Holmes enthused to Dr Watson about the schools the Act had created: 'Light-houses, my boy! Beacons of the future! Capsules with hundreds of bright little seeds in each, out of which will spring the wise, better England of the future.'

47. An obsolete term for uric acid.

48. The breakthrough work of French chemist and microbiologist Louis Pasteur (1822–1895) in treating anthrax (splenic fever), proving his originally controversial case for vaccination and immunology. His first use of a rabies vaccine on a human subject would follow in 1885, a year or two later. Conan Doyle was a medical student when germ theory was still being argued over by physicians, but in the March 1883 issue of the popular magazine *Good Words* he took a public position on these and other medical issues mentioned in his novel in an article called 'Life and Death in the Blood.'

49. This quotation, which may have been taken from some published medical literature of the period, strongly echoes the thesis he was then writing for his M.D. degree from Edinburgh University, 'An Essay upon the vasomotor changes in *tabes dorsalis* and on the influence which is exerted by the sympathetic nervous system in that disease.' The handwritten thesis, dated April 1885, is part of the Edinburgh Research Archive today, and online at www.era.lob.ac.uk/handle/1842/418. Later, in his 1892 novel *Beyond the City*, Conan Doyle wrote: 'Doctor Balthazar Walker was a very well-known name in the medical world. Did not his qualifications, his membership, and the record of his writings fill a long half-column in the "Medical Directory," from his first little paper on the "Gouty Diathesis" in 1859 to his exhaustive treatise upon "Affections of the Vaso-Motor System" in 1884?' Gouty diathesis describes John Smith's affliction; the second topic is a generalized way of describing Conan Doyle's own M.D. thesis.

50. Conan Doyle's 'Life and Death in the Blood' presaged the 1966 science-fiction movie *Fantastic Voyage* in its examination of the human bloodstream and its microbial content: 'Had a man the power of reducing himself to the size of less than one-thousandth part of an inch, and should he, while of this microscopic structure, convey himself through the coats of a living artery, how strange the sight that would meet his eye!'

51. At medical school in Edinburgh a few years before, Conan Doyle had witnessed the war over germ theory, with Dr Joseph Lister there in the forefront by applying antisepsis in surgery. Later Conan Doyle recorded it in a piece of medical fiction, 'His First Operation,' based on his student days: 'It's Lister's antiseptic spray,' one characters says, 'and Archer's one of the carbolic-acid men. Hayes is the leader of the cleanliness-and-cold-water school, and they all hate each other like poison.' Conan Doyle sided with the 'carbolic-acid men.'

52. Robert Koch's work on tuberculosis would draw Conan Doyle to Berlin in 1890, where he filed a report on the findings for W.T. Stead's *Review of Reviews*. In his autobiography, Conan Doyle would suggest that the trip had been an impulsive decision – 'I could give no clear reason,' he wrote – but the reference here suggests a long-standing interest in Koch's work. In any case, the trip to Berlin

would mark a significant turning point, as it introduced him to a Harley Street specialist named Malcolm Morris, who 'assured me that I was wasting my life in the provinces and had too small a field for my activities.' On his return to Southsea, he decided to sell his medical practice. 'I came back a changed man,' he recalled. 'I had spread my wings and had felt something of the powers within me.'

53. The Tugela is a river in the Zulu country of South Africa.

54. Conan Doyle's next comment, 'cast your mind back to your dear old mother, who strove so long and worked so hard to find the means for your education,' is autobiographical. While he opposed women's suffrage most of his life, out of concern for the divisiveness within families he felt it might cause, the influence of certain women in his life was very strong. Foremost among them was his Irish-born mother, Mary Foley Doyle, who held the family together and ensured her children's educations (seven surviving into adulthood) when Charles Doyle collapsed into alcoholism. Conan Doyle also idolized his older sister Annette, who until her early death from influenza in 1890 was sending home her wages as a governess in Lisbon for the family's benefit, followed in this by his younger sisters Lottie and Connie.

55. Here Conan Doyle may have been thinking about something else, his on-again, off-again romance with a young lady named Elmore Weldon. This was a case in which his mother felt there *was* room for improvement, in Miss Weldon's attitude toward her son and herself. In time Conan Doyle came to agree, and let the relationship end. In 1885 he married Louisa Hawkins, known as 'Touie,' the 27-year-old sister of an adolescent patient of his who had died.

56. Sikes was the villainous brute in Charles Dickens's *Oliver Twist*. Conan Doyle had not thought this way about the matter when he was a medical student, according to his 1910 speech at St Mary's Hospital, London, where his son Kingsley was a student. 'The Romance of Medicine' looked back at the less spiritual, more determinist views of medicine in the 1870s: 'We looked upon mind and spirit as secretions from the brain in the same way as bile was a secretion of the liver. Brain centres explained everything, and if you could find and stimulate the centre of holiness you would produce a saint – but if your electrode slipped, and you got on to the centre of brutality, you would evolve a Bill Sikes. That was, roughly, the point of view of the more advanced spirits among us. I can clearly see now as I look back, that this frame of mind was largely a protest and a reaction against transcendental dogmas which had no likelihood either in reason or in science. Swinging away from dogma, we lost all grip upon spirituality, confusing two things which have little connection with each other – indeed, my experience is that the less the dogma the greater the spirituality. We talked about laws, and how all things were done by immutable law, and thought that was profound and final.'

57. Not, of course, the path China actually took, and in a few years Conan Doyle would also see growing rivalry with Kaiser Wilhelm's Germany, leading to the World War in which Conan Doyle would participate as a Home Guardsman, propagandist, war correspondent and historian. He lived long enough (dying in July 1930) to see the work of the victors in that war undone by the rise of Bolshevism and Fascism in Europe.

58. Farid ud-Din 'Attar, author, among other works, of *The Conference of the Birds*, from which the line quoted comes, and one of the 'Big Six' ancient Persian poets in whom Conan Doyle took an interest, as we shall see further on.

59. Sir John Lubbock (1834–1913) was a British banker and amateur scientist (and champion of Darwin), well known for his observations of ants and other insects. He would go on in another two years to co-found the Great Books movement, and his 1887 book *The Pleasures of Life*, rhapsodizing about books and his personal library, may have been a model for Conan Doyle's own such book *Through the Magic Door*.

60. Conan Doyle was not a Freemason at the time he composed this manuscript, though he became one in Southsea in 1887, if not long an active one. The thought expressed here, though, remained part of his literary vocabulary. 'There is a wonderful sympathy and freemasonry among horsy men,' Sherlock Holmes tells Dr Watson in the 1891 story 'A Scandal in Bohemia.'

61. Samuel Carter Hall (1800–1889) was a prominent art critic and journalist whose memoirs *Retrospect of a Long Life* had just been published in 1883. While Conan Doyle was no artist himself, in terms of painting and other visual arts, his father, uncles and grandfather John Doyle were all notable artists, and he was attuned to their world. Hall's advocacy of art he approved of was influential, but he was also known for a sanctimonious character that got him frequently satirized, including supposedly by Dickens as the model for Pecksniff in *Martin Chuzzlewit*. Not all saw him as virtuous as Conan Doyle did.

62. In the name 'Dr Pontiphobus' Conan Doyle may have been suggesting 'aversion to Pontiffs,' or Popes – i.e., the Roman Catholic Church, which he had renounced without having embraced Dr Pontiphobus's Anglican Church instead.

63. James (not John) Anthony Froude, the English writer and biographer of Carlyle, whose falling away from the Oxford Movement and the Roman Catholic Church had been an inspiration for Conan Doyle's own defection from the Church as a youth – causing discord with his relatives, if not his mother.

64. The German Romantic writer Johann Paul Richter (1763–1825), often called Jean Paul, was noted for his love of nature, and cited by Sherlock Holmes in his second tale, *The Sign of the Four* (1889), about the beauty of the dawn.

65. 'Against stupidity the gods themselves fight in vain.' Conan Doyle acquired his French from his mother, an avid reader of French periodicals, but studied German in school, including a year between Stonyhurst College and Edinburgh University at a Jesuit school in Feldkirch, Austria.

66. Perhaps Mark Twain, a favourite of Conan Doyle's, but he was an enthusiastic reader of others as well, and after joining the Portsmouth Literary & Scientific Society thought about giving a talk there on 'The American Humourists.' (He made his debut there instead on 'The Arctic Seas.')

67. Apparently a reference to the Salvation Army, founded in London in 1865 by William Booth, a former Methodist minister.

68. A Roman Catholic order founded in France in the late twelfth century.

69. In the first chapter of *A Study in Scarlet*, written in 1885 and published in 1887, Dr Watson related his service as an Army surgeon in Afghanistan: 'The campaign brought honours and promotion to many, but for me it had nothing but misfortune and disaster. I was removed from my brigade and attached to the Berkshires, with whom I served at the fatal battle of Maiwand. There I was struck on the shoulder by a Jezail bullet, which shattered the bone and grazed the subclavian artery. I should have fallen into the hands of the murderous Ghazis not it not been for the devotion and courage shown by Murray, my orderly, who threw me across a pack-horse, and succeeded in bringing me safely to the British lines.' (Although sometimes in the Sherlock Holmes stories Watson's wound seems

to have been in his leg.) After being invalided home, Watson is introduced to Holmes, and agrees to share lodgings with him.

70. Usually spelled Afridi, a Pashtun tribe of Afghanistan, frequent foes of the British.

71. Or perhaps an expression of Social Darwinism, a concept in circulation since the 1870s, in the application of Charles Darwin's theory of biological evolution to social phenomena.

72. A passage perhaps suggested by the crusted mud and creeping fog of the famous atmospheric opening of Charles Dickens's *Bleak House*.

73. Devotees of Sherlock Holmes will be reminded of the 1903 story 'The Adventure of the Empty House,' by which Conan Doyle brought Holmes back from the dead, and once again into the pages of the *Strand Magazine*. Here Conan Doyle, a great admirer of Poe, may have had in mind Poe's description of Roderick Usher's decaying family mansion, in 'The Fall of the House of Usher,' of 'vacant eye-like windows,' though Conan Doyle included a characteristic touch of medical knowledge.

74. A coloured lithograph done in oil colours on canvas to approximate an oil painting.

75. 'the fancy': Regency slang (*circa* 1800) for its prizefighting world. ('nose-ender': a straight blow to the nose.) In *The Sign of the Four*, an ex-pug recognizing Sherlock Holmes as a former amateur opponent says, 'Ah, you're one that has wasted your gifts, you have! You might have aimed high, if you had joined the fancy.' In 1896 Conan Doyle, avid amateur boxer himself, wrote an historical novel about that Regency life, *Rodney Stone*.

76. Some commentators on Conan Doyle's life have taken remarks like these in his fiction as reflecting turmoil and even violence in his own family, given his father's alcoholism, but there is no actual evidence of such incidents, and some testimony against it. Part of Conan Doyle's earlier work for Dr Reginald Ratcliffe Hoare had been in the slums of Birmingham, where he had witnessed that dimension of life. He entirely approved of women having power in marriages, and in later years became president and spokesman of the Divorce Law Reform Union, to make divorces easier and less disadvantageous for women to obtain.

77. Australia's gold-rush started at Ballarat, Victoria, in 1851. Conan Doyle was interested in it and the upheavals that resulted: the crime in his 1891 Sherlock Holmes story 'The Boscombe Valley Mystery' has a Ballarat gold-rush background, and in *The Sign of the Four* Conan Doyle had already placed Dr Watson there in his earlier days: 'It looks as though all the moles in England had been let loose in it. I have seen something of the sort on the side of a hill near Ballarat where the prospectors had been at work.' Conan Doyle himself did not visit Australia until 1920, during a Spiritualist speaking tour there and in New Zealand.

78. Young Conan Doyle was convinced that, despite his profession and his conformity to its canons, his was a Bohemian disposition. Recounting his first visit to London, staying with his uncles and aunts, he wrote in *Memories and Adventures*: 'I fear that I was too Bohemian for them and they too conventional for me.' He felt he was Bohemian by nature, living a Bohemian life in Southsea, and transferred this posture to Sherlock Holmes, who Dr Watson said 'loathed every form of society with his whole Bohemian soul.'

79. An idea Conan Doyle reworked considerably but recognizably later for *Rodney Stone*: 'Well I remember his thin, upright figure and the way in which he jauntily twirled his little cane; for cold and hunger could not cast him down, though we

knew that he had his share of both. Yet he was so proud and had such a grand manner of talking, that no one dared to offer him a cloak or a meal. I can see his face now, with a flush over each craggy cheek-bone when the butcher made him the present of some ribs of beef. He could not but take it, and yet whilst he was stalking off he threw a proud glance over his shoulder at the butcher, and he said, "Monsieur, I have a dog!" Yet it was Monsieur Rudin and not his dog who looked plumper for a week to come.'

80. Conan Doyle, an enthusiastic reader of American humourists, was perhaps ill advised to turn to Ralph Waldo Emerson, America's foremost nineteenth-century philosopher and essayist, on the subject. Emerson (1803–1882) had a very earnest attitude toward life and its burdens, and his essay 'The Comic,' from his 1876 collection *Letters and Social Aims*, seems determined to convince readers that there is little reason in life to laugh.

81. William Rutherford, a physiologist who experimented with methods of measuring 'the rapidity of nerve-force,' was one of Conan Doyle's most memorable professors at Edinburgh. Later, in *Memories and Adventures*, the author recalled 'his Assyrian beard, his prodigious voice, his enormous chest and his singular manner' in creating Professor Challenger in *The Lost World*. 'He fascinated and awed us,' Conan Doyle said. 'He would sometimes start his lecture before he reached the classroom, so that we would hear a booming voice saying: "There are valves in the veins," or some other information, when his desk was still empty. He was, I fear, a ruthless vivisector, and though I have always recognized that a minimum of painless vivisection is necessary, and far more justifiable than the eating of meat as food, I am glad that the law was made more stringent so as to restrain such men as he.'

82. Samuel Clemens (1835–1910), known to the world as Mark Twain. Conan Doyle once lamented to a reporter that he had 'never had the good fortune to run across Mark Twain' in his travels in America (speaking of a three-month lecture tour there in 1894), but in June 1907 he attended a London dinner for Clemens given by US ambassador Whitelaw Reid, when Clemens came to England to receive an honorary degree from Oxford.

83. "'They say that genius is an infinite capacity for taking pains," [Holmes] remarked with a smile. "It's a very bad definition, but it does apply to detective work."' (*A Study in Scarlet*). Carlyle's remark comes from his *Life of Frederick the Great*.

84. Here, one suspects, he is thinking of Dr Joseph Bell of Edinburgh, under whom Conan Doyle worked as a medical student. Bell had uncanny powers of observation and deduction as a physician, and also as a forensic witness in criminal trials, and Conan Doyle gave him public credit for the Sherlock Holmes method depicted in his tales. 'His intuitive powers were simply marvellous,' Conan Doyle said, describing the manner in which Bell could 'at a glance' construct a patient's entire medical history and personal background.

85. Sir Edwin Arnold (1832–1904), English journalist (reporting on Asia, notably) and poet. The reference to 'instinct is memory' may come from his essay 'The Indian Upanishads,' collected in his 1896 book *East and West, Being Papers Reprinted from the Daily Telegraph*: 'the marvels of what we call instinct, which looks like a pre-natal memory.' Arnold goes on to give several examples, the first perhaps suggesting the one Conan Doyle gives in his next paragraph: 'the jungle-chicken pecking its food, distinguishing wholesome from unfit seeds, on the very first day of its emergence from the egg.'

86. Henry Crabb Robinson (1775–1867), English journalist, lawyer and antiquarian,

whose posthumously published *Diary, Reminiscences and Correspondence* is a significant source about the leading figures of England's Romantic movement.

87. A viewpoint Conan Doyle would shortly transfer to Sherlock Holmes in *A Study in Scarlet*: 'I consider that a man's brain originally is like a little empty attic, and you have to stock it with such furniture as you choose. A fool takes in all the lumber of every sort that he comes across, so that the knowledge which might be useful to him gets crowded out, or at best is jumbled up with a lot of other things, so that he has a difficulty in laying his hands upon it. Now the skilful workman is very careful indeed as to what he takes into his brain-attic. He will have nothing but the tools which may help him in doing his work, but of these he has a large assortment, and all in the most perfect order. It is a mistake to think that that little room has elastic walls and can distend to any extent. Depend upon it there comes a time when for every addition of knowledge you forget something that you knew before. It is of the highest importance, therefore, not to have useless facts elbowing out the useful ones.' (See also p. 74.) Conan Doyle had Sherlock Holmes repeat his brain-attic view again in the 1891 story 'The Five Orange Pips.' (Not that he was consistent: the time Holmes quotes Carlyle without attribution in *A Study in Scarlet*, Watson had previously said: 'Upon my quoting Thomas Carlyle, he inquired in the naïvest way who he might be and what he had done.')

88. It was Watson's consternation at discovering Holmes did not know the earth revolved around the sun, nor cared, that prompted the dissertation in the preceding note. When Watson protested 'But the Solar System!' Holmes replied: 'What the deuce is it to me? You say that we go round the sun. If we went round the moon it would make not a pennyworth of difference to me or to my work.' (At the time, Watson did not yet know what that work was.)

89. William Parsons, third Earl Rosse (1800–1867), an astronomer who in 1845 built the nineteenth century's largest telescope, known as the Leviathan.

90. Dr Turner has suddenly become Dr Julep for the remainder of the manuscript, perhaps a sarcastic or even snide reference to the word's Middle English meaning, of a sweet syrupy drink to which medicine can be added.

91. Perhaps reflecting his physician's apprehension about his father Charles Doyle's trajectory. Because of worsening alcoholism he was sent for treatment to an Aberdeenshire institution called Blairerno, the first of several asylums for increasingly serious mental problems from which Charles Doyle never re-emerged, dying at the Crichton Royal Hospital in Dumfries, Scotland, in 1892.

92. Three novels by Charles Reade (1814–1884), also the author of *The Cloister and the Hearth*, mentioned in Conan Doyle's next sentence along with several other mid-Victorian novels as 'fine examples of pure storytelling' – none of which has endured as well as his own 1901 Sherlock Holmes novel *The Hound of the Baskervilles* or his 1910 science-fiction novel *The Lost World* as fine examples of pure storytelling.

93. Conan Doyle would return to this theme in *Through the Magic Door*. 'This I am sure of,' he says, 'that there are far fewer supremely good short stories than there are supremely good long books. It takes more exquisite skill to carve the cameo than the statue. But the strangest thing is that the two excellences seem to be separate and even antagonistic. Skill in the one by no means ensures skill in the other.'

94. Conan Doyle was to become one of the most successful short-story writers in his own or other languages, but here he praises predecessors immensely important

to him. Poe he once called 'the supreme original short story writer of all time,' saying on another occasion that 'If every man who receives a cheque for a story which owes its springs to Poe were to pay tithe to a monument for the master, he would have a pyramid as big as that of Cheops.' Bret Harte, another American writer, was counted by Conan Doyle as a strong influence, including on his first Sherlock Holmes novel *A Study in Scarlet*, with its flashback set in the American West in a style reminiscent of Harte. Stevenson, the Scottish writer with whom he corresponded late in that writer's life, was a great favourite: his 'Pavilion on the Links' Conan Doyle had described, before knowing Stevenson was its author (it was published in *The Cornhill* in 1880 without a by-line), as 'a splendid story … one of the most powerful I ever read.'

95. Conan Doyle would probably have said his hobby was sports. He was an avid cricketer, footballer and boxer, and played many other games as well in the course of an active lifetime. Many similes and allusions in his fiction come from sports and their worlds.

96. Conan Doyle's famous citation of Hafiz occurs in the 1891 story 'A Case of Identity,' in which Holmes tells Watson: 'You may remember the old Persian saying, "There is danger for him who taketh the tiger cub, and danger also for whoso snatches a delusion from a woman." There is as much sense in Hafiz as in Horace, and as much knowledge of the world.' And Conan Doyle not only read Persian poets, but about them as well; Sir William Jones and Baron von Hammer-Purgstall were referenced again as authorities in his 1889 potboiler *The Mystery of Cloomber*. But according to Elizabeth T. Gray, Jr, noted translator of Hafiz, the proverb in 'A Case of Identity' is not by him, nor by any of the other Persian poets Conan Doyle mentions above.

97. Jules Barthélemy-Saint-Hilaire (1805–1895), author of a number of mid-nineteenth-century books about Buddhism, as well as with works on many other subjects.

98. Conan Doyle would not have described himself as a mathematician, but did harbour some warm feeling for the fifth proposition of Euclid. 'Detection is, or ought to be, an exact science, and should be treated in the same cold and unemotional manner,' Holmes told Dr Watson peevishly in *The Sign of the Four* about the latter's account of *A Study in Scarlet*: 'You have attempted to tinge it with romanticism, which produces much the same effect as if you worked a love-story or an elopement into the fifth proposition of Euclid.'

99. A malediction cited in Laurence Sterne's *Tristam Shandy*. The French-born Ernulphus (1040–1124) was a one-time prior of Canterbury Cathedral who later became Bishop of Rochester, with the entire lengthy, comprehensive curse contained in the medieval manuscript *Textus Roffensis*. Conan Doyle would invoke this curse again in *The Stark Munro Letters*: 'I must mention no names,' Dr Stark Munro declares at one stage, 'for the curse of Ernulphus, which includes eight and forty minor imprecations, be upon the head of the man who kisses and tells.'

100. Uncle Toby is a leading character from *Tristam Shandy*.

101. Conan Doyle was a happy composer of doggerel verse his entire life, but in the area of medicine his father had suggested, as a mnemonic device, writing verse about facts he needed to remember, and Conan Doyle had written many along the lines above during medical school, into his copy of *The Essentials of Materica Medica and Therapeutics* by Alfred Baring Garrod (Longmans, 1877), now at the University of Texas. About the effects of quinine, for example, Conan Doyle wrote: 'In ears a sound, in eyes a flash, / Vomit, headache, nausea, rash, /

Thirst, no hunger, heart goes slower, / Then if he goes and swallows more, / He'll die from cardiac paralysis, / Shown by a post mortem analysis.'

102. A simile he would use again to describe literary characters; in the 1904 Sherlock Holmes story 'The Adventure of Black Peter,' for example: 'The first who entered was a little Ribston pippin of a man with ruddy cheeks and fluffy white side-whiskers.'

103. Perhaps citing Sir John Bowring's religious poem of that title, but more likely Goethe's. ('Goethe is always pithy,' Conan Doyle once had Sherlock Holmes observe.)

104. An infection of the tip of the finger.

105. Where Conan Doyle, as a medical student, had clerked for Dr Joseph Bell.

106. 'Hard and forceful punishment,' abolished in Great Britain in 1772.

107. A closed four-passenger horse-drawn carriage.

108. '"You have erred, perhaps," [Sherlock Holmes] observed, taking up a glowing cinder with the tongs and lighting with it the long cherry-wood pipe which was wont to replace his clay when he was in a disputatious rather than a meditative mood,' said Dr Watson in the 1892 story 'The Adventure of the Copper Beeches.' Long cherry-wood pipes make appearances in a number of Conan Doyle's tales in these years, another his 1890 novel *The Firm of Girdlestone*.

109. Not many, perhaps, would have chosen to stay in a boarding house kept by Charlotte Corday, after she stabbed French Revolutionary leader Jean-Paul Marat to death in his bath.

110. John William Colenso (1814–1883), a controversial Anglican theologian in whom the young Conan Doyle was interested. To the dismay of his fellow churchmen and many laymen, Colenso had challenged the historicity of the Pentateuch, the first five books of the Old Testament. Three years earlier, while preparing for his Arctic voyage aboard the whaler *Hope* in February 1880, Conan Doyle reported to his mother: 'The chief engineer came up from the coal hole last night & engaged me upon Darwinism, in the moonlight on deck. I overthrew him with great slaughter but then he took me on to Colenso's objections to the Pentateuch and got rather the best of me there.'

111. A term out of phrenology, the pseudo-science popular in the first half of the nineteenth century, and not a unique figure of speech. It occurs, for example in Vol. 18 of *Bentley's Miscellany* for 1845, in an instalment of *Glimpses and Mysteries*, a series by Alfred Crowquill, entitled 'The Old Woman at the Corner.' Perhaps not entirely coincidently, *Bentley's Miscellany* at the time was running a multi-part series about seventeenth-century murderess the Marquise de Brinvilliers, whose crimes were the inspiration in 1903 for one of Conan Doyle's most famous *Tales of Terror and Mystery*, 'The Leather Funnel.' *Bentley's Miscellany* was edited by Charles Dickens originally, and in 1868 merged with *Temple Bar* magazine, publisher of some of Conan Doyle's earliest stories. *Bentley's Miscellany* was also one of the first to carry Edgar Allan Poe's tales in Britain, beginning with four in 1840 including 'The Fall of the House of Usher.'

112. 'But no woman has a voice,' states Conan Doyle's 'liberated-woman' Mrs Westmacott in his 1892 novel *Beyond the City*. 'Consider that the women are a majority in the nation. Yet if there was a question of legislation upon which all the women were agreed upon one side and all the men upon the other, it would appear that the matter was settled unanimously when more than half the population were opposed to it. Is that right?' Yet Conan Doyle never supported women's suffrage. He counted himself a Liberal Unionist in politics, running for

Parliament unsuccessfully twice, in 1900 and 1906, in Edinburgh and northern English constituencies.

113. Usually spelled Stuart.

114. Joseph Smith, founder of the Mormon Church in America, a subject of interest to Conan Doyle who gave *A Study in Scarlet* a strong Mormon sub-plot of revenge against two fugitive Mormons responsible for the death of the killer's beloved years before.

115. Conan Doyle refers to the so-called Tichbourne Claimant case of the 1860s and '70s, one of British jurisprudence's longest, not finally settled until 1873 when Conan Doyle was a schoolboy at Stonyhurst College. The heir to a moneyed title, who had been missing since 1854, apparently reappeared in 1866, but was challenged by members of the family and eventually proven to be a former butcher from Wagga Wagga, Australia, named Arthur Orton. Conan Doyle and his schoolmates had taken an interest in the case during its 1872–1873 perjury trial phase because the missing heir had been a Stonyhurst graduate, and a favourite teacher of Conan Doyle's had been called to testify.

116. English inventor Samuel Rowbotham (1816–1884), whose Zetetic Society promoting his astronomical theory was succeeded by the still-existing Flat Earth Society.

117. Karl Wilhelm Friedrich Schlegel (1772–1829), German Romantic poet and scholar.

118. 'A fool always finds one still more foolish to admire him' (Nicolas Boileau-Despréaux). Conan Doyle would give the quote to Sherlock Holmes in *A Study in Scarlet*.

119. Chamonix in the French Alps and the Rigi mountain in Switzerland.

120. A phrase that could have had a number of origins for Conan Doyle in his reading, including *Reason: The Only Oracle of Man, A Compendious System of Natural Religion*, by Ethan Allen (Boston, 1854), or from Freemasonry.

121. Conan Doyle was seriously interested in psychic phenomena by the time he wrote this novel, experimenting with various forms of it in Southsea under the guidance of his friend, retired Major-General Alfred Drayson. While he sounds convinced here, and would sound quite won over in a letter to the psychic journal *Light*, in its 2 July 1887 issue (see *Arthur Conan Doyle: A Life in Letters*, p. 269), his actual conviction to spiritualism would wax and wane for many years, until he finally committed to that faith in 1916.

122. A trace of the theosophist Alfred Percy Sinnett (1840–1921). 'I read Sinnett's *Occult World* and afterwards with even greater admiration I read his fine exposition in *Esoteric Buddhism*, a most notable book,' Conan Doyle wrote in *Memories and Adventures*: 'I also met him, for he was an old friend of General Drayson's, and I was impressed by his conversation.' In *Occult World* Sinnett wrote a good deal reflected in Conan Doyle's ideas, including: 'It is not physical phenomena, but these universal ideas, that we study; as to comprehend the former, we have first to understand the latter. They touch man's true position in the universe.'

123. From Ralph Waldo Emerson's conclusion to his 1836 essay *Nature*, first published anonymously, which laid the foundation of Transcendualist doctrine. Conan Doyle quotes it incompletely here, dropping these exultant sentences with 104 words about the perfect world to come, and abridging the final sentence which actually reads: 'The kingdom of men over nature, which cometh not with observation, – a dominion such as now is beyond his dream of God, – he shall enter without more wonder than the blind man feels who is gradually restored to perfect sight.'

124. Sentiments such as these never left Conan Doyle, especially after witnessing war at first hand as a correspondent for the *Westminster Gazette* during Kitchener's campaign on the Nile in 1896, and as an army field surgeon in South Africa during the Boer War in 1900. (His brother Innes from an early age aimed at an Army career, rising during the World War to the rank of brigadier.) After the Boer War, Conan Doyle became part of the military reform movement that followed, to the irritation of the War Office. In 1914, before the outbreak of the First World War, he published a story called 'Danger!' that warned of the peril posed to Britain by German submarines. When the World War began, he also sent the Admiralty further unwelcome life-saving ideas, like inflatable rubber belts for sailors. 'We can spare the ships,' he declared; 'We can't spare the men.'

125. Once again (and not for the last time) reflecting the young Conan Doyle's belief that he was a Bohemian personality living a Bohemian life. 'When shall I marry, and *who?*' he asked his mother in June 1882, but in fact his letters home from Southsea these first years mention going to dances of various kinds (at one, getting so drunk he had proposed to every unmarried woman present, he claimed), playing on several local sports teams, expanding his circle of professional colleagues, joining the Portsmouth Literary & Scientific Society and giving a presentation on 'The Arctic Seas,' constantly writing and submitting stories to the magazines, and hosting friends from out of town, along with seeing to his younger brother Innes's welfare, and sparring with income tax commissioners.

126. 'To appreciate a woman one has to be out of sight of one for six months,' he wrote in *Memories and Adventures* about his six months at sea aboard the Arctic whaler *Hope* in 1880: 'I can well remember that as we rounded the north of Scotland on our return we dipped our flag to the lighthouse, being only some hundreds of yards from the shore. A figure emerged to answer our salute, and the excited whisper ran through the ship, "It's a wumman!" … She was well over fifty, short skirts and sea boots – but she was a "wumman." "Anything in a mutch!" the sailors used to say, and I was of the same way of thinking.'

127. In fact Conan Doyle and some friends of his in Southsea were conducting experiments in mind-reading around this time, as part of their interest in psychic phenomena. He would give Sherlock Holmes seeming mind-reading powers in a number of stories, beginning with 'The Cardboard Box' in 1893. '"You remember," said he, "that some little time ago when I read you the passage in one of Poe's sketches in which a close reasoner follows the unspoken thoughts of his companion, you were inclined to treat the matter as a mere *tour-de-force* of the author. On my remarking that I was constantly in the habit of doing the same thing you expressed incredulity."' Dr Watson was pleased and impressed on that occasion, but reacted more peevishly on others.

128. Elizabeth Thompson (1846–1933), well-known as a painter of historical and military battle subjects. Conan Doyle had heard her lecture on art in London in 1878. Rosa Bonheur (1822–1899) was perhaps the most famous female painter of the nineteenth century, best known for her pastoral scenes.

129. The view expressed here, however grating to modern ears, was perhaps more John Smith's attitude than Conan Doyle's, for it does not seem to be the view he took from or about his own mother and sisters. In his fiction, too, Conan Doyle took delight in strong, independent women. In 'The Doctors of Hoyland,' an 1894 story in Jerome K. Jerome's magazine *The Idler*, Dr James Ripley meets fierce competition from a lady doctor whose very existence seems a 'blasphemy' to him. She proves the superior practitioner, however, and Dr Ripley finds himself

falling in love in spite of himself. In time, after she has saved his leg following a riding accident, he proposes marriage. 'What,' the prospective bride mocks, 'and unite the practices?' And the crest-fallen Dr Ripley sees his hopes dashed. 'If I had known what was passing in your mind I should have told you earlier that I intended to devote my life entirely to science,' she tells him. 'There are many women with a capacity for marriage, but few with a taste for biology.' Even before this was written, Conan Doyle had seen his fourteen-years-younger sister Ida prove to be the scholar of the family, their brother Innes marvelling to him that Ida at fifteen was 'doing all sorts of wonders,' including winning 'a certificate which allows her to teach science in a national school and to buy 32s worth of books and send the bill to the government.'

130. Perhaps suggested by a fable that Aristophanes tells in Plato's *Symposium*.

131. Quoted in 'A New View of Mormonism' by James Barclay in the January 1884 issue of the London periodical *The Nineteenth Century* (pp. 167–84). Thus this was very fresh reading on Conan Doyle's part, which informed also the Mormon background for *A Study in Scarlet* the following year. In the same issue is a lengthy article about 'Life in a Medieval Monastery' (Augustus Jessopp), perhaps a seed of his historical novel *The White Company*, researched and written while Conan Doyle was still in Southsea and completed there in July 1890.

132. Charles Marlow in Oliver Goldsmith's 1773 classic *She Stoops to Conquer*.

133. A reference from Ralph Waldo Emerson's 1879 essay *Society and Solitude*, the person unnamed but identified as a humourist of considerable intelligence who had lost confidence in his ability to succeed in the social world.

134. Conan Doyle speaks for himself here about Turgenev's *Fathers and Sons*, a book that had impressed him and that he recommended to others, saying for example in a letter home 'Did the Dr. [Bryan Charles Waller of Edinburgh, a one-time mentor] get "Fathers & Sons." I think Tourguenieff is grand – he is so unconventional and so strong.' Yevgeny Vasil'evich Bazarov, mentioned below (as Bazarof) is the novel's nihilist figure, a young man who (like Conan Doyle) was planning a medical career for himself.

135. Conan Doyle would use Russian nihilism and revolutionism against Tsarist autocracy as the theme for his 1904 Sherlock Holmes story 'The Adventure of the Golden Pince-Nez.'

136. Wenzel Anton, Prince of Kaunitz-Rietberg (1711–1794).

137. *The Voyage and Travels of Sir John Maundeville*, published originally in the fourteenth century, was a work of uncertain authorship that had influenced many readers, including Christopher Columbus.

138. Conan Doyle had long read deeply into American history through historians like Francis Parkman, and had romantic views of it informed by writers like James Fenimore Cooper. More than the average Briton of his day, he believed in the importance of ties between the two countries based on language, blood and shared history, and for the dedication of his 1890 novel *The White Company* about the late English Middle Ages, a novel he believed then and later to be his masterpiece, he wrote: 'To the hope of the future, the reunion of the English-speaking races, this little chronicle of our common ancestry is inscribed.'

139. Francis Jeffrey, Scottish critic (1773–1850), who did miss the mark in this instance.

140. 'In the middle of things you will go most safely.' From Ovid's *Metamorphoses*.

141. Top of the line in Dr Conan Doyle's day, from E. Hartnack & Co. of Potsdam and Paris.

142. John Knox (1510–1572), leader of Scotland's Protestant Reformation. One of

Conan Doyle's hard-headed Scots in *The Mystery of Cloomber* would declare that she 'didna' think muckle o' John Knox,' and obviously neither did Conan Doyle himself.

143. 'No fools so wearisome as those who have some wit' (Rochefoucauld, and yet another aphorism that would be voiced by Sherlock Holmes, this time in *The Sign of the Four*).

144. William Paley (1743–1805), sometimes called 'Darwin's theological father.' In May 1884, about the time this was written, Conan Doyle remarked in an article in the *British Journal of Photography*, 'Easter Sunday with the Camera,' that he and his companions were 'coated with dust and dry as if we had swallowed Paley's *Evidences of Christianity*.'

145. It is not known whether this episode is based on a real visit Conan Doyle had from a parish cleric. This episode was transferred to his 1895 novel *The Stark Munro Letters* with only minor changes. Based on that appearance, the late Geoffrey Stavert, in *A Study in Southsea: From Bush Villas to Baker Street* (Portsmouth, 1987), speculated that there may have been such a one by the Rev. Charles Russell Tompkins of St Jude's Church, Southsea.

146. *The Nineteenth Century* was a monthly magazine of public affairs founded in 1877 by the architect and editor Sir James Knowles, who had a particular interest in the conflict between science and religion. Conan Doyle was not only a reader of it (see note 131 above), but at least once a contributor in his Southsea days, an article in its August 1888 issue entitled 'On the Geographical Distribution of British Intellect.'

147. This quotation is not part of the curate's visit in *The Stark Munro Letters*, but does appear elsewhere in that novel, directly attributed to Carlyle (as it is indirectly here).

148. Conan Doyle, who served in South Africa in 1900 as a volunteer British Army field surgeon during the Boer War, had the same disappointment when he tried to join the Army in 1914, at the beginning of the World War. He enlisted in the Home Guard instead, also serving as a war correspondent and historian of the British campaign in France later during the war.

149. Gilbert & Sullivan were and are household names in music; the House of Rimmel was a cosmetics company founded in London by Eugene Rimmel in 1834. 'There are seventy-five perfumes, which it is very necessary that a criminal expert should be able to distinguish from each other,' Sherlock Holmes was to remark in *The Hound of the Baskervilles*.

150. Slang for British soldiers, immortalized by Rudyard Kipling's poem 'Tommy' in *Barrack-Room Ballads*.

151. American poet James Russell Lowell (1819–1891), though the lines are not rendered correctly here; they read 'But somehow, when we'd fit and whipped, I ollers found the thanks / Got kind o' lodged afore they came as low down as the ranks.'

152. Published in a longer and more polished version, and with the sub-title 'A Ballad of '82,' in Conan Doyle's poetry collection *Songs of Action* in 1898.

153. In Conan Doyle's 1912 novel *The Lost World*, as Professor Challenger and his companions ready themselves for a winner-take-all battle, the sportsman and soldier of fortune Lord John Roxton tells the others: 'They'll have something to excite them if they put us up. The "Last Stand of the Greys" won't be in it.' And then without attribution Roxton finishes by quoting from this very poem' of Conan Doyle's: '"With their rifles grasped in their stiffened hands / 'mid a ring of the dead and dying," as some fathead sings.'